madness

chaos fuel
book two

Amy Booker

By

Amy Booker

Published by Renaissan Publishing Limited, Cuyahoga Falls, Ohio

www.amybookerauthor.com

RENAISSAN
PUBLISHING
LIMITED

author's note

If you've read my previous books, you'll know the chapter names are all song titles. Music has been an integral part of my life and always sets the mood for my writing. Whether it's the overall energy of a song, the lyrics, or even the title, that tone carries through into my written words on the page. The playlist and a link can be found at the back of each book, or you can find them on my website: www.amybookerauthor.com.

"Optimism is the madness of insisting that all is well when we are miserable."

-Voltaire.

"when love is forfeit
the fingerprints left on your heart
sting, and sear into immeasurable depths

an indelible reminder that you are a fool."

- Renaissan.

one
nothing ever after

Dakota

The pounding in my head matches the insistent knocking at my bedroom door. It's got to be another bad dream. I groan, burying my face deeper into the pillow, internally willing the noise to stop. But it doesn't. If anything, it grows louder and more urgent.

"Dakota. Come on, man, open the fuck up."

Connor. My best friend and roommate. *God damn it.*

My stomach churns as fragments of last night filter through the haze in my mind.

Shit. What have I done?

"I swear to God, if you don't answer, I'm breaking this fucking door down."

I force my eyes open, wincing slightly at the harsh daylight hitting me as it streams through the gap in my curtains. My tongue feels like sandpaper, and the taste...*ugh*. I swallow hard, fighting back a wave of nausea. I haven't felt this bad in fucking years. But then again, I haven't...

"I'm up," I croak, my voice barely audible. I clear my throat and try again. "I'm up. Fuck."

The knocking ceases, replaced by Connor's muffled voice. "You better be. You said Chaos Fuel's got that interview today. Well, it's in a fucking hour."

Fuck. The *Rolling Stone* interview.

My heart starts to race as I push myself up, the room spinning around me. I squint at the nightstand, searching for my phone. Instead, my gaze lands on an empty Angel's Envy bottle and my breath catches in my throat. There's a small bag with remnants of white powder next to it. I barely remember buying either of them, let alone using them. That's probably for the best.

Three years. I've been clean for three years, and now...

A sob builds in my chest as the full weight of what I've done crashes over me. Three years to the day since I lost Chloe. Three years of fighting to stay clean, honor her memory, and be the person she'd always believed I could be. Hoped I could be. *We* could be.

All of it, gone in one fucking moment of weakness.

My hand shakes as I reach for the bag, desperate to get rid of the evidence. But as my fingers close around it, a wave of longing washes over me.

Just a little something to take the edge off...

No.

I clench my jaw, stumbling to my bathroom. With trembling hands, I dump the bag into the toilet and flush, watching as my temporary insanity swirls away.

I grip the edge of the sink, forcing myself to look in the mirror. Bloodshot eyes stare back at me, ringed by dark circles. My usually clean-shaven face is shadowed with stubble, and my long black hair is a fucking mess.

"What would she think of you now?" I whisper to my reflection.

The answer comes without warning, her voice as clear in my mind as if she were standing right next to me. *"I'd think you're hurting, babe. But you're stronger than this. You've come so far."*

I squeeze my eyes shut, a tear almost escaping. It's a near thing, but I shake it off. I may be a weak piece of shit, but I'm not about to be fucking pathetic on top of it. It's a weird place to draw the line, and I know it, but I have to start somewhere. If hearing ghosts in my head of my dead wife doesn't tell me I need a line to not cross, I don't know what would be.

Another sharp knock on the bedroom door jolts me back to reality. "Dakota. Seriously, man, you gotta go."

I splash cold water on my face, trying to pull myself together. "Yeah, give me five fucking minutes. Christ."

My mind races as I rush through a shower and throw on the first clean clothes I find. Chaos Fuel is on the verge of breaking big. Our latest single is climbing the mainstream charts, and today's interview could be a serious game-changer for us. I can't let them down.

Can't let Chloe down.

But as I stare at an old bottle of painkillers in my medicine cabinet, I wonder if I haven't already done just that. This bottle was supposed to be my talisman. The temptation I triumphed over every day. The touchstone that kept me clean. My reminder of the slippery slope I teeter on the top of every day. The slope I just dove head-first down last night.

The slope that took Chloe from me.

It could have been worse, I try to convince myself. *I could have done a lot worse.*

This was just a little hiccup. I'm fine. I'm totally fine. I can handle it. Outside of my pounding headache, I'm doing alright. I slipped in private, alone, and nobody got hurt. Right?

In fact, the painkillers in this bottle would probably help right now. I need to appear 'normal' for the interview with *Rolling Stone*, not hungover like a typical asshole rockstar.

This is it, though. No more than this. I know my limits and am well aware that I fucked that up last night. It doesn't have to define me going forward. After this, I can stop. The anniversary of Chloe's death hit me harder than I thought it would, that's all. I'm allowed my grief. I just need to make it through today.

Just today.

I dry-swallow two pills, praying they'll fix this hangover. With one last glance in the mirror, making sure I don't meet my own eyes, I toss the empty bourbon bottle in my backpack, steel myself, and open the bedroom door.

Connor stands there, arms crossed, worry etched across his face. "Jesus, you look like hell."

I force a wry smile. "Thanks, man. Just what every

rockstar wants to hear before an interview with *Rolling Stone*."

Connor's eyes narrow, searching my face. "You okay? I know what day it is. Sorry I wasn't here last night."

For a split second, I consider coming clean. Telling Connor everything. But the words stick in my throat. Instead, I clap my friend on the shoulder as I brush past him.

"I'm fine. Just slept like shit. I'll grab a coffee on the way."

As I put on my sunglasses and head out, I silently vow to myself that last night will be a one-off. I'll get back on track. For the band. For myself.

For Chloe.

But deep down, a small voice whispers that it might already be too late.

two
holding out for
a hero

Lauren

"Lauren, we need to talk."

My cousin Shannon's voice drifts up the stairs as I'm wrestling a brush through my tangled dark brown hair. I check my watch and stifle a groan. It's barely 5:30 AM, and I've got exactly ten minutes before I need to leave for my shift at Sunny's Diner. I usually work dinner only, but I'm covering for someone on vacation this week. My tired eyes are not going to earn me any stellar tips today, I can tell already.

"Can it wait?" I call back, wincing as I hit a particularly stubborn knot. "I'm running late as it is."

There's a pause, then the sound of footsteps in the hall. Shannon appears in my doorway, her red hair wild from sleep, cradling a mug of coffee. The serious look on her face makes my stomach clench.

"It's about Seattle," she says, and my heart sinks. I've been dreading this conversation for weeks.

I set down the brush and turn to face her. "You're moving back, aren't you?"

Shannon nods, her green eyes apologetic. "I got a call from my agent yesterday. There's a part in a new series filming up there. It's not huge, but it's steady work for at least a season. And who knows, it might get picked up for another if we're lucky. It's kind of a rom-com. You're gonna love it."

"That's great, Shannon," I say, forcing a smile. And it is great, for her. She's been chasing her acting dream for years, scraping by on bit parts and commercials. She deserves this break.

But the selfish part of me wants to beg her to stay in LA. Without Shannon, I don't know how I'll manage. She's been my rock since my boyfriend Miles died, helping with my nearly three-year-old son Roman, and splitting the rent on this tiny house.

"I want you to come with me," Shannon blurts out. "You and Roman. We could get a place together in Seattle. It'd be just like here, but maybe with better opportunities for both of us."

I turn back to the mirror, avoiding her hopeful gaze. "I don't know, Shannon. Seattle is..."

"Where your parents are," she finishes softly. "I know it's complicated, but maybe it's time you guys mended fences?"

The mention of my parents makes me tense. Their disapproval at my choosing to stay with Miles in LA when I got pregnant, their thinly veiled 'I told you so' when he eventually disappeared and died from an overdose... The thought of facing their judgment again makes my chest tighten.

"I'll think about it," I promise, even though the very idea of returning to Seattle makes my stomach churn. "But right now, I really need to get to work."

Shannon nods, stepping aside to let me pass. "Oh, I almost forgot. Roman was a bit fussy last night. I think he might be coming down with something."

Of course. Just what I need on top of everything else. "Thanks for letting me know. I'll stop by the pharmacy on my way home after the lunch crowd dies down."

After throwing my hair into a ponytail, I peek in on Roman, still sleeping soundly. Putting the back of my hand on his forehead carefully so as not to wake him, I note that he does feel a little warm. Hopefully, it's just a cold and not another ear infection.

As I head down the hall, I can feel Shannon's eyes on me. I know she means well, but the idea of uprooting our lives, of facing my parents' criticism, just isn't something I want to deal with. I still have plans here in LA. Still have dreams of my own.

I grab my keys and bag, pausing at the front door. The house is quiet, except for Roman's muffled snores from his room. It's not much, but it's ours. The thought of leaving it behind makes my heart hurt.

I step further into our tiny living room, taking in the toys scattered across the faded carpet. The secondhand couch sags in the middle, covered with a bright throw to hide the worn spots. Roman's artwork adorns the walls, taped up haphazardly, bringing splashes of color to the otherwise dull rental-beige paint. The kitchen is visible through an archway, dishes piled in the sink, and a calendar on the fridge covered in scribbled appointments and reminders.

But then I see the stack of bills on the kitchen counter and think of the long hours at the diner with measly tips that barely keep us afloat. Maybe Shannon's right. Maybe a fresh start is precisely what we need.

I shake my head, pushing the thoughts aside. I can't deal with this now. I've got a shift to get through, a potentially sick toddler to tend to, and a mountain of other worries to ignore.

As I step out into the pre-dawn chill, I take a deep breath. *One day at a time, Lauren. That's all you can do.*

But as I start my ancient car, Miles' voice comes through the stereo system as it automatically pairs to my phone's last playlist, an old Earth Sign song that makes my heart ache even more. I quickly turn it off, but the damage is done. Tears prick at my eyes as I back out of the driveway.

He's been gone exactly three years now, and it still hits me like a punch to the gut every time I hear his voice. Will it ever get easier?

With a sigh, I point the car towards Sunny's Diner. Time to put on my waitress smile and pretend everything's fine. I can't afford to fall apart, not here, not now. And I certainly can't afford to let my parents' judgment dictate my life again. But with Shannon now leaving, do I have a choice?

Honestly, though, what do I have keeping me here in

LA? Just bad memories and ghosts. But then, Seattle's not exactly 'home sweet home' either. I need a better reason to stay, other than it's slightly better than another bad place. My dream of nursing school could happen anywhere, I guess.

Come on, powers that be, help me out here. Give me a reason to stay or go. Make up my mind for me.

three
light in life

Dakota

I shift uncomfortably in the plush hotel chair, trying to ignore the pounding in my head. The *Rolling Stone* interviewer, a sharp-eyed woman in her thirties, clicks her pen and smiles at us. I force myself to breathe evenly, to appear calm and collected. I've already forgotten her name. I always do.

Just another day in the life of a rockstar, right?

The penthouse suite we're in is all luxury and fucking intimidating – thick carpets that swallow our footsteps, heavy curtains framing floor-to-ceiling windows with a million-dollar view of the LA skyline. Our armchairs are arranged in a semi-circle, facing a sleek coffee table where the reporter's recorder sits like a ticking time bomb. At least three cameras are pointing at us, with boom mics stationed over our heads.

I can do this. I can do this.

"Let's start with your journey, Dakota," she begins.

"You joined Chaos Fuel in quite an unusual way. Can you tell us more about that?"

Jesus Christ. Why does she have to fucking start with me?

I hesitate for a moment, my hand unconsciously tightening around my water bottle. "It's pretty wild, actually," I say, my voice a little rough. I clear my throat and continue, "I saw their post online about needing a new bassist, and I figured, why not? Sent in a video of me playing one of their songs, and somehow, out of thousands of submissions, they picked me."

Our lead singer, Brad, leans forward, eager to jump in. Always our front man. Mr. Charisma. "It wasn't just 'somehow,'" he insists, his long blonde hair swaying as he shakes his head. "Dakota absolutely killed it. We'd been through so many bassists, but when we saw his video, we knew he was the missing piece."

I feel a flush of pride at Brad's words, but it's mixed with a twinge of guilt. If only they knew how close I came to falling apart last night. Actually, no. I *did* fall apart last night. I just hope I put myself together enough for no one to notice today.

The interviewer nods, jotting down notes even though the cameras recording this whole thing. "And you've been touring with the band for a year now. How has that experience been?"

Fuck. Why is she focusing so much on me? Today of all days?

"It's been incredible," I say, and I mean it. Despite everything, being on stage with these guys is the closest thing to pure joy I've felt in years. "Every show is a rush. The energy from the crowd, the connection with the guys. It's everything I dreamed of."

The conversation continues as she peppers the rest of the band with questions and then shifts to our latest single, with Brad explaining the inspiration behind the lyrics. "It's really about resilience," he says passionately. "About facing your demons and coming out stronger."

I feel my throat tighten at his words. I helped write that song. Hell, I help write *all* the Chaos Fuel songs with me and Brad sharing lyrical duties. If only he knew how relevant that song is right now. I take a sip of water, trying to stay present.

"Dakota," the interviewer turns back to me yet again, "how do you feel your style has influenced the band's sound over the past year?"

I relax a little at this question. Music, I know. Music, I can talk about. "I like to think I've brought a bit more edge to the low end," I say, trying not to sound too cocky. "The guys have been great about letting me experiment with different techniques and sounds."

Stefan jumps in this time, his lanky frame stretching out to slap me upside the head playfully. "He's being modest. Dakota's basslines have taken our songs to a whole new level."

The praise should make me feel good, but instead, it just adds to the pressure I'm already feeling. I force a smile and nod my thanks at him.

As the interview appears to wind down, the reporter asks about our upcoming album and tour. "We're in full prep mode," Emmett says, twirling a drumstick while flashing a crooked grin. He's been almost normal the entire interview. I'd expected at least a few oddball jokes to fly out of his mouth. He must realize the importance of this. "Lots of rehearsals, lots of planning. We want to give our fans the best show possible."

"And lots of team bonding," Brad adds with his own grin. "We're like a family now, and that closeness comes through in our performances."

Family. The word hits me like a punch in the fucking throat, reminding me of Chloe, of the family we could have been. I blink hard, forcing the morose thoughts away.

Just keep it together a bit longer. You can do this.

The reporter pauses, her pen hovering over her notepad. Her eyes flick to me, then away, as if steeling herself. Nervous, almost. She shifts in her seat uncomfortably, and my chest tightens with anxiety.

Don't do it. Please don't do it. Not today.

"One more thing, Dakota," she begins, her tone softer than before. "My research uncovered that today marks a significant anniversary for you. Would you be willing to talk about your late wife, Chloe?"

Fuck me.

The question hits me like a physical blow. The room suddenly feels too small, too hot, and way too fucking crowded. It's as if all the air has been sucked out of the room. I can feel the eyes of my bandmates on me, and Ian, our manager, takes a step forward from the sidelines, ready to jump in if I need him to. They know about

Chloe, of course, but we've never really talked about it. Not like this. It's just not something I do.

I swallow hard, my throat dry again. The water I've been downing like it's going out of style isn't working. "I... I'm not sure what to say," I manage, my voice barely above a whisper. The plastic bottle in my hand crinkles as I grip it tighter. I give Ian a brief glance, unsure if I need him or not.

"It's been three years today, hasn't it?" the reporter presses gently. "How has that loss influenced your music, if at all?"

Flashbacks of that night invade my mind like lightning bolts. Chloe's moment of weakness. The phone call from the police. The funeral. They're like movie clips with no sound or real context, but together, they tell the tragic story. And it suddenly feels fresh all over again.

For a split second, I consider deflecting, changing the subject. But something in me fractures. Maybe my brain is still foggy, or maybe it's the weight of the secret I'm carrying, but suddenly, I want to talk about her. I wave to Ian that it's okay.

"Chloe was..." I start, then stop, searching for the right thing to say. "She was everything. My anchor, my muse. Losing her... it broke something in me. But it also drove me. Every note I play, every song I write, it's all for her. It's how I keep her memory alive."

I can feel the tension in the room, thick and heavy. The silence is almost deafening. This isn't what they expected, this raw honesty. But now that I've started, I can't seem to stop.

"The thing is," I continue, avoiding everyone's gaze, but my voice gains strength, "grief isn't something you just fucking get over. It's something you learn to carry. And some days, like today, it's heavier than others. But music... music helps lighten the load."

After another weighted silence, the reporter nods, her eyes sympathetic. "Thank you for sharing that. I'm sure your words will resonate with many of our readers who have experienced loss."

As she moves deftly on to the next question, I catch Brad's eye. He gives me a slight nod, a silent show of support. I appreciate it, but I've never talked about Chloe publicly like this before, and I'm not sure how to feel about it. It's like the wound I haphazardly opened last night in private is somehow festering now that it's exposed to open air. It almost feels like a mistake to have said anything. Maybe I should have kept it to myself like I always do.

When the interview finally wraps up, the reporter stands to leave, thanking us for our time, and I let out a deep breath. We made it through. I made it through. But as I watch the crew pack up their equipment, I can't shake the feeling that they all saw more than I wanted them to. The equipment's being packed away, but I feel like I'm the one being dismantled. Beneath the surface of the lucky bassist who got his big break, they saw a man barely holding his shit together.

How long before everyone else sees it, too?

four
blackbird

Dakota

I push through the glass door of Sunny's Diner, the bell jingling overhead. The familiar scent of coffee and burgers mingles with industrial cleaner, starkly contrasting the posh hotel we just left. Cracked red vinyl booths and gleaming chrome accents greet us, the diner's worn charm a welcome comfort.

"You good?" Stefan asks, his brow furrowed with concern.

I nod, forcing a smile I don't feel. To be honest, I haven't felt much today. "Yeah, just need some grease and caffeine."

The truth is, I need something to fucking do other than go home and dwell on shit.

I can still feel the reporter's eyes on me, searching for the things I don't share. Did she buy the story about my red eyes being from allergies? Did my hands shake when I took those millions of sips of water?

Even after a year with Chaos Fuel, I still feel like the

'new guy.' Being picked from an internet fan contest has branded me an amateur despite years of playing in LA bands. The reporter bringing up my background during the interview might help establish my legitimacy, but the pressure to prove myself every day is still there.

We slide into a booth, and I grab a menu, more to hide behind than to actually read. We've been coming here often enough; I know it by heart.

"Well, if it isn't my favorite rockstars," a cheerful voice says, and I lower my menu to see Jen, one of the regular waitresses. "The usual for you boys?"

Stefan nods enthusiastically, but before I can respond, another waitress approaches. She's new - or at least, I've never seen her here before. Her dark brown hair is pulled back in a long ponytail, and there's a weariness in her hazel eyes that speaks of long nights and longer days.

"Sorry, Jen," she says, her voice soft but firm. "This is my section today."

Jen shrugs good-naturedly. "All yours, Lauren. Just don't let Dakota here charm you into extra fries like he does with me."

I feel my face heat up, but Lauren just nods politely. "I'll keep that in mind," she says, turning to us. "So, what can I get for you?"

Stefan rattles off his order, and I manage to get mine out without stumbling. Something about Lauren catches my attention, but I can't quite put my finger on it. It's not attraction, exactly, more like a vague sense of familiarity.

As Lauren jots down our orders, a small silver locket around her neck catches the light as she leaves. For a moment, I'm transported back to last night, to the glint of silver on my nightstand. Chloe's wedding ring, which I've kept all these years. I usually always keep it in my pocket. Today, of all days, I forgot.

"You okay, Dakota?" Stefan's voice snaps me back to reality. "You look... off."

I shake my head, trying to clear it. "Yeah, just thinking about the interview. Hope I didn't say anything stupid."

Stefan laughs, running a hand through his short blonde hair. "Nah, you were great. The fans are gonna eat it up. I think it went really well, actually. She asked good questions."

I can't help but shrug at that. I'm not sure all the questions were that great. In fact, I'm still conflicted about talking about Chloe at all.

Stefan leans in, lowering his voice. "But man, I gotta ask... are you okay? That stuff about Chloe... We've never heard you talk about her like that before."

And there it is. At least I wasn't the only one affected by it. I tense up, my fingers tightening around my coffee mug. "I'm fine," I say, maybe too quickly. "It just... caught me off guard, you know? I didn't think that would come up, to be honest."

Stefan nods, his expression a mix of concern and understanding. "Yeah, I get it. We were all pretty surprised. But hey, if you ever want to talk about it..."

I force a smile. "Thanks, but I'm good. Really."

The lie curdles something deep inside of me, but Stefan, while a great guy, wouldn't understand. He still parties. Still lives like he's invincible. Nothing can touch him. I haven't gotten that close with him for that very reason.

If I'm truly close with anyone in the band, it's Brad. But we write lyrics together, so he sees my feelings written down all the time. He used to ask about them but has come to realize over time that I don't really like talking about shit. So, he's kind of stopped asking, which is fine with me. It hasn't hindered our relationship at all.

Stefan eyes me dubiously across the table for a minute, and I start to worry he's seeing through my lies about being okay. If only he knew how close I'd come to blowing it all up last night. How close I still am.

"So, changing the subject, but not really... what do you think about the way the interviewer kept focusing on you? It's like she couldn't get enough of the 'internet contest winner makes it big' angle."

I shrug, trying to appear nonchalant. "I guess it's a good story. Better than 'Dude plays bass, joins band' anyway."

"True," Stefan chuckles. "But seriously, you've more than proven yourself this past year. You're one of us now, man. Don't let anyone make you feel otherwise."

His words hit me deeper than I expected. I swallow hard, nodding. "Thanks, man. I appreciate that."

Before Stefan can say anything else, movement catches my eye. Lauren approaches our table, a welcome distraction from the heaviness of our conversation. She returns with Stefan's drink, setting it down carefully. As she refills my coffee, her sleeve rides up slightly, revealing a small tattoo of a treble clef on her wrist.

"Music fan?" I ask, nodding towards her wrist.

She glances down as if surprised to see it there. "Oh, yeah," she says, a hint of something like sadness or nostalgia creeping into her voice. "It's... complicated."

Our eyes meet briefly, and there's a flicker of something between us. Not recognition, exactly, but a sort of shared understanding. Like we're both carrying weights we can't quite put down.

"Complicated. I get that," I say, more to myself than to her.

Lauren nods, her expression neutral. "Your food will be out soon," she says, turning and hurrying away.

As she walks back to the kitchen, I find my gaze following her. There's a story there, I realize. Or maybe a song. Not that it's any of my business.

"Earth to Dakota," Stefan says, kicking me under the table. "You with me? We need to talk about the upcoming tour schedule. Please don't make me bunk with Emmett the entire trip this time. That dude is getting out of hand with his fucking pranks."

I tear my gaze away from Lauren, focusing on my bandmate. "Yeah, sorry. Where were we?"

As we dive into a discussion about our upcoming tour, I can't shake the feeling that something's shifted. Not in any big, dramatic way. Just a ripple. A minor disturbance in the world around me.

And for the first time in a while, I find myself curious

about something other than the next album or show. I'm curious about someone else. Lauren, with her weary eyes and that mysterious treble clef tattoo. It's not a lot to go on, but it's different. Right now, being different feels like a step in the right direction.

Or maybe she's just the distraction I'm looking for. Something or someone to take my mind off everything.

Everyone.

Three years since Chloe. Maybe it's about time I moved on. Or at least tried to. And maybe this unexpected curiosity about a cute waitress is the first step. It's been so long since I've felt even a flicker of interest in anyone else.

But am I ready for that? Or am I just setting myself up for another fall?

five
the prophecy

Lauren

T he lunch rush is finally winding down, and I lean against the counter, stealing a moment to catch my breath. My feet ache, I'm exhausted, and a dull throb behind my eyes promises a full-blown headache later. But none of that matters when I think about getting home to Roman.

As I'm wiping down the counter, I feel a presence nearby. I look up to see Dakota, the bassist from Chaos Fuel, standing there. His friend is nowhere to be seen and must have left. I've barely paid attention like I should with everything on my mind today.

"Everything okay?" I ask, straightening up, a familiar wariness creeping into my voice. LA is full of beautiful people, and Dakota is one of them. Even as tired as he looks, he's gorgeous. Tall. Long hair. Tattoos. Handsome. Unfortunately, he's just my type.

I catch myself admiring how his t-shirt clings to his shoulders, then immediately chastise myself. This is exactly how it started with Miles. But Dakota seems different somehow.

No. I can't afford to think like that again.

He shakes his head, a slight smile on his face. "No, just... wanted to say thanks. For the service, I mean."

"Oh," I say, surprised. "Well, you're welcome. It's my job, after all."

There's a moment of awkward silence, and I find myself studying him. Up close, I can see the shadows under his eyes, and the slight tremor in his hands. He *really* looks tired. Worn. It's all too familiar, and a knot forms in my stomach. I've seen this before with Miles. The small signs I chose to ignore until it was too late. Now, I find myself looking for them. I could be wrong, though. He could just really be tired.

"So," he says finally, "I don't think I've seen you here before. Do you usually work different hours?"

I nod, keeping my tone professional. "Yeah, I'm usually on the dinner shift. Covering for Lynn, who's off today." I don't say that I *have* seen him before, more than a few times. He's just always been in a different section than mine. Why point out how unremarkable I apparently am to him?

"Ah," he says, nodding. There's something in his eyes that catches my attention. Curiosity, maybe? No. I've learned the hard way not to read too much into someone's interest.

"Must be a change of pace," he continues, clearly trying to keep the conversation going.

For a moment, I'm tempted to let my guard down.

To see him as just another person, not a potential threat to my hard-earned stability. But then I remember Miles, remember all the promises, all the disappointments, and especially the spiral that ended in tragedy. I can't go down that road again with another musician.

I won't.

"It's different," I say with a shrug of my shoulder, my smile polite but distant. "If you'll excuse me, I need to finish up here."

Before he can respond, my phone buzzes in my apron pocket. It's a text from Shannon.

> SHANNON: Roman's fever is definitely up. Can you pick up medicine on your way home?

As I read Shannon's text, all I can think about is Roman's flushed face and how small he looks when he's sick. My heart aches to be with him, to soothe his fever and whisper that everything will be okay. It's been on my mind all morning, but I've been too busy to check on him.

I mentally calculate how much medicine will cost and whether I can squeeze it out of this week's grocery budget. Maybe I can skip lunch for a few days. It's not ideal, but Roman comes first.

Always.

But now I'm conflicted. I'm left with concern for Roman and relief at the excuse to end this interaction. "I'm sorry," I say to Dakota, already untying my apron. "I need to go. My son is sick."

Understanding flashes across his face. "Of course. I don't wanna keep you."

I turn to leave, but his voice stops me. "Hey, Lauren?"

I look back at him, guard firmly in place, purposely hiding my surprise at his knowing my name. Never mind the name tag pinned to my uniform.

"I... I come here pretty often. Maybe I'll see you around again?"

There's something in his tone that strikes me. It's not flirtatious, exactly, but hopeful. For a wild moment, I wonder if this is it. The sign I've been looking for. But then I remember thinking the same about Miles and where that led me. Where that led all of us.

"Maybe," I say, noncommittal. "I'll be back on my usual evening shift tomorrow, though."

He nods, that stupidly attractive slight smile back on his face. "Good to know."

As I hurry out of the diner, my mind is a whirlwind. Roman needs me. Shannon's waiting for an answer about Seattle. The bills are piling up. Nursing school applications are due soon. And now here's Dakota, stirring up memories and fears I've worked hard to bury.

Today is not the day for this.

I slide into my car, gripping the steering wheel tightly. *Deep breaths, Lauren. You've been here before. You know how this story ends.*

But as I pull out of the parking lot, a traitorous voice in the back of my mind whispers: *What if it's different this time?*

I shake my head, trying to get rid of the thought.

Different? How many times did I tell myself that about Miles? How many times did I convince myself that this time, he'd stay clean? That this time, he'd choose us over the drugs and the hardcore lifestyle?

The stoplight turns red, and I pause, watching the dwindling lunch crowd hurry by on the sidewalk. Normal people with normal lives. No addiction, no drama, no ghosts haunting their every decision.

Is that what Seattle could be? A fresh start, away from the memories and the temptation of "what ifs" embodied by men like Dakota? Would we be better off there?

But then I think of Roman, of the life we've built here despite everything. Of the strength I've found in myself, the resilience I never knew I had. I've done that here. In LA.

The light turns green, and I make a decision. I'm not running away. Not yet. I've faced down demons before, and I can do it again. Shannon's move and my financial struggles are just new challenges to overcome.

As I drive, I can't help but glance at the college brochure peeking out of my bag. The nursing program looks perfect, and it offers a chance at a stable career. It's something I've always dreamed of doing. But with our tight budget and my unpredictable schedule, and now Shannon moving out, it feels like a far-off fantasy. Shannon's been my rock, but I can't rely on her forever. Part of me is terrified of her leaving, of losing that support. But another part whispers that maybe it's time I stand on my own two feet and prove to myself that I can do this alone if I have to.

Pulling into the pharmacy parking lot, I feel a newfound determination settling over me. Catching my reflection in the rearview mirror, my eyes are tired, but I recognize a resolve there. It's the same look I had when I decided to keep Roman, when I rebuilt our lives from scratch after Miles died. I've weathered storms before. I can do it again.

I don't know what tomorrow will bring, but I do know this: I'm freaking Lauren Hudson, survivor, mother, and much more than just some rockstar's cautionary tale.

six
spirits high

Dakota

I sit in my parked car outside Sunny's Diner, my hands gripping the steering wheel so tight my knuckles are white. I've been here for twenty minutes, fighting an internal battle that's becoming all too familiar lately.

Part of me - a loud, insistent part - is screaming to just drive away. To go home, lock myself in my room, and lose myself in the oblivion I know is waiting for me there. The anniversary of Chloe's death has passed, but the pain hasn't. It's still raw, still bleeding, and I know exactly how to numb it.

But another part, quieter but somehow stronger, keeps me rooted to this spot. It's the part that's curious about Lauren, the waitress with the tired eyes and the complicated story. The part that, for the first time in three years, feels something other than grief or guilt.

And that scares the shit out of me.

I close my eyes and take a deep breath. *I can do this. It's just a solo dinner. I've done a million of these. It's maybe just a conversation. It doesn't have to mean anything.*

But what if it does?

I shake my head, trying to clear my head. One step at a time, Dakota. Just get out of the fucking car first.

Finally, I force myself to move. I push through the door of Sunny's Diner, the familiar jingle of the bell overhead barely registering. My eyes scan the room, searching for a specific face among the dinner crowd.

There she is – Lauren, moving between tables with practiced ease. Her long dark ponytail swings as she navigates the narrow spaces, and I find my eyes drawn to the graceful curve of her neck. Even in the unflattering diner uniform, there's an understated beauty about her that I hadn't fully appreciated before. The warm glow of the overhead lights catches the hint of gold in her hazel eyes as she smiles at a customer, and I feel my heart rate pick up.

Shit. I'm in trouble already.

I deliberately choose a booth in her section, sliding into the cracked vinyl seat. My fingers drum an anxious rhythm on the laminate tabletop as I wait for her to notice me. It's stupid, really. I'm acting like some lovesick teenager, not a grown man who's seen his share of shit.

When Lauren finally approaches, there's a flicker of recognition in her eyes, quickly masked by professional politeness. "Good evening," she says, pulling out her notepad. "What can I get for you today?"

I clear my throat, suddenly nervous. "Hey, uh, how's your son doing? Is he feeling better?"

Surprise flashes across her face, followed by a guarded look. "He's... better, thank you for asking. The fever broke last night."

I nod, relieved. "That's good to hear. Kids can be pretty resilient, huh?"

A small, genuine smile tugs at the corner of her mouth. "They certainly can be."

There's a moment of awkward silence, and I realize I should probably order something. "Oh, right. Can I get a coffee and the cheeseburger special?"

Lauren jots down my order, her professional mask firmly back in place. But as she turns to leave, I can't help but feel like I've made a tiny crack in her defenses. Maybe my own defenses, too. It's not much, but it's a start.

She returns a few minutes later, setting a steaming mug of coffee in front of me. "Your burger will be out soon," she says, turning to leave.

"Wait," I blurt out before I can stop myself. She pauses, looking at me warily. "I mean, if you have a minute, I'd like to chat."

She glances around the diner. It's not too busy, and I see her weighing her options. Finally, she gives a slight nod and slides into the booth across from me. "I have a few minutes," she says cautiously.

I take a sip of coffee, nearly scalding the inside of my mouth in the process, buying time as I try to think of something to say. I should have had a fucking plan before I started this. I'm not exactly good on the spot. "So, uh, how long have you been working here?"

"A couple years," she replies, her fingers absently

tracing patterns on the tabletop. "It's not glamorous, but it pays the bills."

I nod, understanding all too well the need to make ends meet. But then I start racking my brain, wondering why I never noticed her before. Surely, I should have. Have I been that wrapped up in my own shit? Or maybe it's just that I've been going through the motions for so long, not really seeing anything or anyone around me. It's a sobering thought – how much of life have I missed while I've been drowning in grief and guilt? Lauren's been here the whole time, and it's like I'm seeing her for the first time. It makes me wonder what else I've been blind to all this time.

"And your son... how old is he?"

A soft smile touches her lips, and for a moment, the guarded look in her eyes fades. "Roman is just about to turn three."

The words hit me like a punch to the gut. Three years old. That means he was born right around the time... I swallow hard, pushing back the memory of hospitals and funeral homes. Three years ago, I was losing everything while Lauren was gaining a whole new world.

"That's a great age," I manage to say, even though I have no real experience with kids. My voice sounds strained even to my own ears, but I push on. "Must keep you on your toes."

Lauren chuckles, a warm sound that makes something that's been dead for a long time flutter in my chest. "I assume you have no kids?" When I shake my head no, she continues, "Then you have no idea. He's into everything these days. Curious about the whole world."

As Lauren starts talking about Roman's curiosity, I can't help but wonder what my life would be like now if things had gone differently. Would Chloe and I have had kids by now? The thought sends a sharp pain through my chest, a reminder of all I've lost and all I'll never have.

There's a moment of silence between us that almost feels comfortable, and I find myself wanting to know more. "Is it just you and Roman?" I ask, then immediately regret it when I see her expression close off again.

"Yes," she says simply, and I know I've hit a sensitive topic. Fuck.

"I'm sorry," I backpedal quickly. "I didn't mean to pry."

Lauren shakes her head, her guard sliding back into place. "It's fine. I should get back to work."

As she stands, I feel a panic rising in my chest. I don't want this conversation to end, not like this. "Lauren," I say, and she pauses. "I'm glad Roman is feeling better."

She looks at me for a long moment, tilting her head to the side a little, and I see something shift in her eyes. "Thank you, Dakota," she says softly. "I'll be back with your food soon."

Watching her walk away, I realize I'm in deeper than I thought. And I'm not sure if that terrifies me or thrills me more. The only thing I'm sure of is that I have no clue what the fuck I'm doing.

beach seduction

Lauren

I flip the sign on the door to 'Closed' as the last of the regular customers file out. The diner's usual chatter and clatter fade to a hush, replaced by the soft hum of the refrigerators and the distant buzz of the neon sign outside. The overhead lights seem brighter now even though they're not, casting long shadows across the mostly empty booths and highlighting the smudges on the freshly wiped tables. The air, still heavy with the lingering scents of coffee and grilled food, takes on a different quality—expectant, almost, as if the space itself is exhaling after a long day.

My feet ache, and all I want is to get home to Roman, but my gaze is drawn to the lone figure still occupying a booth in the corner. Dakota has been here for hours, nursing coffee and picking at a slice of pie. His presence in the newly quieted diner seems more pronounced, a focal point in the empty space. The subdued lighting accentuates the sharp angles of his face, his dark hair falling messily over his forehead and shoulders. His fingers, adorned with silver rings, tap an irregular rhythm on the table. Even in his seemingly relaxed posture, a coiled energy about him is like a tightly wound spring. When they flick up to meet mine, his eyes are deep and intense, carrying a weight that seems at odds with his rockstar persona. In this moment, stripped of the stage lights and screaming fans, he looks more human and more intriguing than ever.

I should be annoyed at a customer overstaying their welcome, but instead, I feel a flutter of something else. Curiosity? Anticipation? The twilight hour in the diner suddenly feels charged with possibility.

I can't help but reflect on the evening. Throughout my shift, I'd found myself hyper-aware of his presence. Our eyes had met across the diner more times than I cared to admit, each glance accompanied by a small, almost shy smile from him. Whenever I'd passed by his table, he'd looked up from his coffee, offering a nod or a quiet "How's it going?" It's been ages since anyone has shown that kind of gentle attention, and I'm surprised by how much I enjoyed it.

At one point, during a particularly hectic rush, he'd caught my eye and mimed taking a deep breath. I'd found myself following his lead, feeling some of the tension ease from my shoulders. These little moments, spread throughout the evening, created a strange sense of connection. It was as if we'd been sharing a secret, a quiet understanding of some kind in the middle of the diner's chaos. And despite my best efforts to stay professional and detached, I can't deny that I looked forward to each of those brief interactions.

I try to extricate the strange feelings bubbling up inside me. I don't have time for this. I don't have room in my life for complications.

But as I approach his table, I hear myself saying, "Mind if I join you for a minute?"

He looks up, surprise and something like relief flickering across his face. "Please," he says, gesturing to the seat across from him.

I slide into the booth, suddenly unsure of what to say. Our earlier conversation has been playing on repeat in my mind all evening. The way he asked about Roman, the flash of pain in his eyes when I mentioned my son's age. There's a story there, I'm sure of it.

"So," I start, surprising myself with my boldness, "any particular reason you're still here? We closed ten minutes ago."

Dakota's hand twitches slightly as he reaches for his coffee mug. "Just enjoying the ambiance," he says with a forced laugh that doesn't reach his eyes. "Nah, I guess I just lost track of time. Been working on some lyrics."

I glance at the empty table in front of him, devoid of any writing materials. No pen. No notebook. "Must be all in your head then," I say, not buying his excuse for a second.

He shrugs, not meeting my eyes. "Yeah, sometimes that's how it works." His fingers go back to drumming a restless rhythm on the tabletop, and I notice a slight tremor in his hands that seems to linger.

"Anything you want to share?" I ask, genuinely curious. "I promise I won't steal your next hit song."

That draws a legitimate chuckle from him. "Trust me, you wouldn't want to. It's all pretty raw right now." He pauses, seeming to debate with himself. "It's about... loss. And trying to move forward."

I nod, understanding all too well. "That's a big topic."

"Yeah," he says softly. "It is."

There's a moment of silence between us. I watch Dakota fidget with his empty mug, his movements jittery and unfocused.

"So," he says, clearly trying to change the subject, "how was your shift? Besides having to deal with annoying lingering customers, I mean."

I smile, appreciating his attempt at humor. "Oh, you know. The usual mix of poor tips and ridiculous demands. Nothing I can't handle."

We fall into an easy conversation about the trials and tribulations of the service industry. Dakota's a good listener, asking thoughtful questions and sharing his experiences from his pre-fame days. But I can't help noticing the way his eyes occasionally dart to the exit, or how he can't seem to keep his hands still.

After discussing my job, I decide to shift the conversation. "So, what's it like being in Chaos Fuel? Must be pretty exciting."

He leans back, a flash of pride crossing his face. "It's... intense. Amazing, don't get me wrong, but it's a whole different world."

"I bet," I say, nodding as I try to imagine it. "Do you ever miss your old life? Before all the fame?"

Dakota's quiet for a moment as he thinks about his response. "Sometimes," he admits. "There's a simplicity to anonymity, you know? But I wouldn't trade this opportunity for anything."

I nod, trying to understand the complexity of his feelings. "What about your family? Do they get to see you much with all the touring and stuff?"

His face clouds over slightly. "I, uh... I don't really have much family left. It's mostly just me these days."

"Oh," I say softly, recognizing the pain in his voice. "I'm sorry, I didn't mean to pry."

He shakes his head, offering a small smile. "It's okay. What about you? Besides Roman, I mean. Any family nearby?"

I feel my own walls going up slightly. "Not really. My parents are in Seattle, but we're not close. It's just me and Roman. And Shannon, my roommate. She's my cousin." I pause, glancing at my watch. "Speaking of Roman, I hope he's not giving Shannon too much trouble tonight. He's been going through a phase where he refuses to sleep unless I sing his favorite lullaby."

Dakota leans in, looking genuinely interested. "What's the lullaby?"

I feel my cheeks warm slightly. "'*You Are My Sunshine.*' It's silly, I know, but—"

"It's not silly," Dakota interrupts softly. "It's beautiful. It sounds like you're a good mom."

His words catch me off guard, and I feel a lump form

41

in my throat. I swallow hard, pushing back the unexpected wave of emotion. "Thanks," I manage. "I'm trying to be."

"Sounds like we both know something about being on our own, too," Dakota says, his eyes meeting mine with a look of understanding.

For a moment, we're both quiet, the weight of our shared loneliness hanging between us. Then, surprising myself again, I break the silence. "It's not always easy, is it? Being the one holding everything together?"

Dakota's eyes widen slightly, as if surprised by my candor. "No," he says softly. "No, it's not."

At that moment, I feel a connection with him that goes beyond mere attraction or curiosity. It's a recognition of a kindred spirit, someone who understands the weight of responsibility and loneliness.

But before I can dwell on it too much, I glance at the clock, realizing suddenly how late it's gotten. "I should probably finish closing up," I say reluctantly. "Shannon's probably wondering where I am."

Dakota nods, looking relieved and disappointed at the same time. It's an odd mix of emotions. "Of course. I'm sorry for keeping you."

As we stand, I find myself not wanting the night to end just yet. "Well, I'm working tomorrow night, too," I hear myself say, and I swallow hard. "If you wanted to stop by again, I mean. Maybe bring a notebook next time for those lyrics?"

A small smile touches Dakota's lips, even as his hands

clench and unclench at his sides. "I might just do that," he says softly.

I walk him to the door, and we exchange a slightly awkward goodbye. As I watch him disappear into the night, I can't shake the feeling that there's so much more going on with Dakota than he's letting on. And despite my better judgment, I find myself wanting to know more.

I've been down this road before with musicians. With Miles. The charisma, the intensity, the hint of darkness just below the surface - it's all so familiar. But there's something different about Dakota. Maybe it's how his eyes soften when he talks about family, or how he seems genuinely interested in my life beyond flirting. Or maybe I'm just seeing what I want to see.

Last time, I dove in headfirst, blind to the red flags. This time, I tell myself, I'll be smarter. I'll be careful. But as I remember the warmth in Dakota's smile, and the understanding in his eyes when we talked about loneliness, I can't help but wonder if being careful is even possible anymore.

Turning back to the diner, I start my closing routine. Something catches my eye as I approach Dakota's table to clear it. Tucked partially under the empty coffee mug is a folded bill. My heart skips a beat as I pick it up and unfold it.

It's a hundred-dollar bill.

For a moment, I just stare at it, my mind racing. He paid for his dinner hours ago and tipped me then. A reasonable tip. This is way too much for a few cups of coffee and a slice of pie. I should run after him; tell him he made a mistake. But a small voice in my head reminds me of the pile of bills waiting at home, of Roman's upcoming doctor's appointment tomorrow morning.

I close my eyes, taking a deep breath. When I open them, I carefully fold the bill and slip it into my pocket. As I finish cleaning up, I can't help but smile to myself. It's been a long time since anyone's done something so unexpectedly kind for me.

As I lock up and head to my car, I realize that by inviting Dakota back tomorrow, I'm stepping onto a path I'm not sure I'm ready for. But for the first time in a long time, I'm curious to see where it might lead.

I halt at my car, my breath hitching slightly as my mind races with possibilities and imagined scenarios.

"What the hell am I doing?"

eight
fall eternal

Dakota

I step out of the diner, the cool night air hitting me like a slap to the face. I glance at my car briefly, debating my next move. Ultimately deciding to walk, the conversation with Lauren replays in my head, filling me with both warmth and warning.

What the actual fuck am I doing?

My hands are shaking as I fumble for my phone. I need a distraction, something to keep me from thinking about buying a bottle of whiskey. Or worse.

I scroll through my contacts, desperately seeking someone, anyone, to talk to. Brad's number comes up first, but I hesitate. He'd ask too many questions. Stefan? No, he's probably out partying. I don't need witnesses anyway. Emmett? Fuck, I don't even know what time zone he's in right now. He left for God-knows-where right after our interview with *Rolling Stone*.

We're supposed to be recharging before going back

on the road. A short break before the chaos of another tour.

I'm not recharging. I'm regressing.

The tremors in my hands are getting worse. I can feel the craving building, a familiar ache that's terrifying and tempting.

For a second, I'm thrown back to six months ago, standing on stage at our biggest show. The roar of the crowd, the pulsing lights, the music flowing through me. I remember thinking, *'This is it. This is better than any high.'* I felt invincible then, like I'd finally beaten this thing. Like I'd never need a drink or drug again.

But now, standing on this dark street, that memory feels like it belongs to someone else. Some alternate version of me that had his shit together. The contrast between then and now is so stark it makes me physically ache. How did I go from that guy to this so quickly?

Lauren's face flashes in my mind. Her tired eyes, her gentle smile. The way she looked at me like I was just a fucking person, not a rockstar or an addict or Chloe's widower. For a moment, I felt almost normal.

But that's the problem, isn't it? I'm not normal. I'm a fucking mess, and getting involved with someone like Lauren would only drag her down with me. She's got a kid, for Christ's sake. She doesn't need my fucking baggage.

I can already see how it would play out. At first, it'd be great. I'd be on my best behavior, trying to be the guy she deserves. But sooner or later, the cravings would hit. I'd start lying, sneaking around. Maybe I'd miss her kid's birthday because I'm too hungover. Or worse, show up drunk. I'd see the disappointment in her eyes, and watch as she slowly realizes what a mistake she's made.

And Roman... fuck. That kid deserves better than to have some addict rockstar stumbling in and out of his life. I've seen what that does to a family. I've lived it. I can't do that to them. Lauren's got enough on her plate without having to worry about whether I'm going to fall off the wagon and shatter whatever little stability she's built for herself and her son.

No, it's better this way. Better to keep my distance, to be just another customer at the diner. It's the kindest thing I can do for her, even if it feels like ripping my own heart out. I barely know her, but there was a connection there tonight.

Maybe that's what I'm really afraid of. The crime I'm guilty of. A connection with someone who isn't Chloe. I feel like a fucking traitor already, and all I did was talk to someone.

I find myself walking further with no real destination in mind. Just putting one foot in front of the other, trying to outrun the thoughts in my head. But they're catching up, and fast.

Before I know it, I'm standing outside a liquor store. The neon 'OPEN' sign blinks at me, a beacon in the darkness. It would be so easy. Just one drink to take the edge off. To quiet the noise in my head.

My phone buzzes in my pocket, startling me. For a wild moment, I think it might be Lauren. But it's just a notification from the band's group chat. Some meme Emmett thought was hilarious.

I stare at the screen, my thumb shakily hovering over the call button. I should reach out to someone.

Connor. The guys.

Anyone.

But instead, I find myself pushing open the liquor store door. The bell jingles, eerily similar to the one at Sunny's Diner. I can already feel it haunting me. The sharp scent of alcohol hits me immediately, a mix of stale beer and sweet liquor that makes my mouth water involuntarily. The low hum of the refrigerators joins with the tinny sound of a radio playing softly in the background. It's a sensory overload that's familiar and overwhelming, pulling me in even as a part of me wants to run.

As I walk down the aisle, bottles gleaming under fluorescent lights, I can't shake the feeling that I'm betraying something. Or someone. Lauren's understanding eyes. Chloe's memory. My own hard-won sobriety.

But the pull is too strong. The need to escape, to numb, to forget.

I reach for a bottle, my hand steadier than it's been all night, but it's not my brand. Am I really going to be picky right now? I put the bottle back reluctantly.

Again, fuck it.

"I'm sorry," I whisper, though I'm not sure who I'm apologizing to.

As I approach the counter, keeping my head down so I'm not recognized, I try to convince myself this is just a momentary slip. That I can handle it. Tomorrow, I'll get back on track.

But what if I can't? What if this isn't just another one-time thing? The other night is all the proof I need that this isn't. Was it last night? Or the night before?

Fuck. I'm a mess.

We're on the verge of something huge with Chaos Fuel. One slip-up from me could derail everything we've worked for. I can almost hear Brad's disappointed sigh, see Stefan's worried glances, and feel the weight of Emmett's uncharacteristic silence.

They took a chance on me, the new guy with a mysterious past. They don't know the half of it - the depths I've sunk to, the battles I fight every day. They see the talent and the dedication but not the demons. If I fuck this up, if they find out what I'm really capable of... it's not just my life I'm messing with. It's theirs, too. Our shot at the big time, gone because I couldn't keep it together.

The thought should be enough to make me walk out of this store. But instead, it just makes me want to drink more, to drown out the guilt and the fear of letting them down.

But deep down, I know.

This is how it starts.

Again.

The cashier eyes me warily as I approach, probably wondering if he should ask for an autograph or call security. I keep my head down, my voice low as I mutter my order.

"Bottle of Angel's Envy, please."

The words taste like ash in my mouth, but I force them out anyway. As he turns to grab the bottle, I have one last chance to walk away, to prove to myself that I'm stronger than this.

I don't take it.

Instead, I pull out my wallet, the leather smooth and expensive against my trembling fingers. A gift from the record label for our chart-topping single.

If only they could see me now.

The bottle lands on the counter with a dull thud that seems to echo in my chest.

One step closer to the edge.

"That'll be $62.99," the cashier says, his voice oddly distant.

I hand over four crisp twenties, the exchange feeling surreal. Like I'm watching someone else go through the motions.

"Keep the change," I mutter, grabbing the bottle nestled in a discreet brown paper bag.

Its weight in my hand is both comforting and terrifying. A lifeline and a noose all at once.

As I push open the door, the stupid bell jingling mockingly behind me, I realize I've made my choice. For better or worse.

Tonight, I drown.

nine
time is running out

Lauren

The dinner rush is in full swing, but I can't stop my eyes from darting to the door every time the bell jingles. Each time, my heart does a little flip, only to sink when it's not him walking through.

Dakota.

I try my best to just freaking focus on the orders in front of me. What am I doing? I barely know the guy. But after last night's conversation, I can't help but feel like maybe, just maybe, there's a connection there.

"Order up for table six!" Jen's voice cuts through my thoughts.

I grab the plates, forcing a smile as I deliver them to a family of four. The little boy at the table reminds me of Roman, and I feel a pang of guilt. I should be home with him, not here hoping for a glimpse of some rockstar who probably doesn't even remember my name.

Roman's fever finally broke, but the doctor confirmed another ear infection. Third one this year. The antibiotics are going to stretch our budget even thinner, and with Shannon's bombshell about when she's moving to Seattle, I'm running out of time to get my life straightened out.

"Three weeks," she'd said over coffee, not quite meeting my eyes. "The show starts filming in three weeks. I have to go, Lauren."

I'd nodded, trying to be supportive, but inside, I was panicking. How am I going to manage rent on my own? Childcare? School? It's all too much.

The bell jingles again, and I look up, hope rising despite myself. But it's just another regular, sliding into his usual stool at the counter.

No Dakota.

It's stupid to be disappointed. He probably said he'd come back just to be polite. Why would he actually want to spend time in some run-down diner when he could be anywhere else?

"Earth to Lauren," Jen says, waving a hand in front of my face. "You okay? You seem distracted."

I force a laugh, hoping it doesn't sound as hollow as it feels. "Yeah, just tired. Roman's been sick."

Jen nods sympathetically. "Poor little guy. Hope he feels better soon."

As she walks away, I can't help but wonder what Dakota's doing right now. Is he at some fancy Hollywood party? In the recording studio? Or maybe he's just at home, having completely forgotten about the waitress he talked to last night. Or, better yet, he's out with some hot model or something. That's probably more likely.

The night wears on, and the weight in my chest grows heavier with each passing hour. By closing time, I'm full of disappointment and self-directed anger. How could I be so naive? To think that someone like him would be interested in someone like me?

As I wipe down the last table, I make a decision. No more daydreaming about rockstars. I need to focus on what's real. Roman. Finding a way to make ends meet without Shannon. Nursing school. Improving our future. That's what matters.

Not some guy who couldn't even be bothered to show up.

The last customer finally leaves, and I flip the sign to "Closed" with a sigh of relief. My feet ache, and I only want to get home to Roman. As I gather my things and head out the back door, I'm already planning tomorrow's budget in my head. Maybe if I cut back on—

I freeze mid-step. There's a figure leaning against my car, illuminated by the dim parking lot lights. My heart races, fear and adrenaline coursing through me until I recognize the silhouette.

Dakota.

He looks up as I approach, and even in the poor lighting, I can see he's a mess. His hair is disheveled, dark circles under his eyes, and his clothes look slept in. But his eyes are clear, alert.

"Lauren," he says, straightening up. His tall frame

casts a long shadow. "I'm sorry, I didn't mean to scare you."

I approach cautiously, my earlier disappointment warring with concern and a hint of anger. "What are you doing here?"

He runs a hand through his hair, a gesture that seems more nervous than rockstar cool. "I... I wanted to apologize for not coming in earlier. I didn't want to bother you while you were working, but I really wanted to see you."

I cross my arms, trying to ignore the flutter in my chest at his words. "So, you decided to lurk in the parking lot instead?"

He winces. "Yeah, I realize now how creepy that sounds. I'm sorry. I just... I wondered if we could talk for a while? If you're not too tired, that is."

I should say no. I should get in my car and drive home to my son. But something in Dakota's eyes, a vulnerability I hadn't seen before, makes me hesitate.

"Talk about what?" I ask, softer this time.

He shrugs, looking almost shy. "Anything. Everything. I just... I had a rough night, and talking to you yesterday, it helped. More than you know."

I study him for a moment, weighing my options. Finally, I sigh. "There's a 24-hour diner a few blocks from here. We can grab a coffee if you want."

Relief washes over his face. "Yeah, that'd be great. Thanks."

We head towards the diner, but I can't help but wonder what I'm getting myself into. Despite my better judgment, despite the voice in my head telling me to be careful, I find myself looking forward to whatever conversation lies ahead.

Maybe, just maybe, I'm not the only one who felt that connection last night.

As we walk, I pull out my phone. "Just give me a second," I say to Dakota, quickly typing out a text to Shannon.

> ME: Grabbing coffee with a friend. Be home a bit late. How's Roman?

I hit send, then turn my attention back to Dakota. He's walking beside me, hands shoved in his pockets, looking almost nervous. It's such a contrast to the confident rockstar image that I can't help but feel intrigued.

"So," I begin, breaking the silence, "rough night?"

He lets out a dry chuckle. "You could say that. I almost did something I would have regretted."

I nod, not pushing for details. "But you didn't?"

"No," he says softly. "I didn't. But it was close."

We walk in silence for a moment, the weight of his unspoken struggle hanging between us. My phone buzzes, and I glance down.

> SHANNON: He's fine. Still no fever. Have fun, but be safe! x

I smile slightly, tucking the phone away.

"How's your son?" Dakota asks, catching me off guard. "Roman, right? Is he feeling better?"

The fact that he remembered surprises me. "Yeah, Roman. He's doing okay. But it turns out he has another ear infection. Nothing we haven't dealt with before, though."

Dakota nods, looking genuinely concerned. "That's tough. Kids are resilient, but still... it must be hard on you both."

"It is," I admit. "But we manage. Always do."

We're quiet for another moment, and then Dakota speaks again. "Lauren, I want you to know that I meant to come in earlier. I was there, actually. Sat in my car for about an hour, trying to work up the courage."

I raise an eyebrow. "Courage? To enter a diner?"

He laughs, but it's a self-deprecating sound. "Crazy, right? I can perform in front of thousands, but the thought of walking in there, seeing you... it terrified me."

"Why?" I ask, genuinely curious.

He stops walking, turning to face me. His eyes meet mine, and I'm struck by their intensity. "Because you make me feel... real. Not like some stupid fucking rock-star, or some screwed-up addict, but just... me. And that's both amazing and terrifying."

The word 'addict' hits me like a physical blow. Suddenly, I'm back three years ago, the phone call telling me Miles was dead. The sleepless nights, the broken promises, the constant fear - it all comes rushing back.

A voice in my head screams at me to run, to protect myself and Roman from going through that hell again. Red flags are waving frantically in my mind. I should end this right now, turn around, and go home to my son.

But as I look at Dakota, I see something I never saw in Miles - a vulnerability, an openness about his struggle.

He's not hiding it or making excuses. And despite every instinct telling me to flee, I find myself curious about his story.

Still, I can't ignore the warning bells. I need to be careful, for Roman's sake, if not my own.

I take a deep breath, trying to keep my voice steady. "Addict, huh? That's a lot to process. I appreciate your honesty, but I hope you understand that I need to be careful. I have Roman to think about."

He nods, understanding and disappointment in his eyes. "Of course. I get it. I shouldn't have dumped all that on you right then. I'm sorry."

Before I can respond, the diner's neon sign comes into view. "We're here," I say, gesturing towards the entrance, grateful for the distraction.

I feel his hand brush against mine as we walk towards the door. It might be accidental, but the brief contact sends conflicting sparks and anxiety through me that I can't ignore.

Whatever happens next, I have a feeling this night is going to change things. I just hope I have the strength to handle it - and the wisdom to know when to walk away if I need to.

ten
help

Dakota

The fluorescent lights of the diner feel harsh after the dim glow of the streetlamps. Lauren slides into a booth, and I follow, trying to ignore the tremor in my hands. I'm sober, but the cravings are still there, lurking beneath the surface.

A tired-looking waitress approaches, and Lauren orders coffee for both of us. As the waitress walks away, an awkward silence settles over us.

"So," Lauren says finally, her fingers nervously tracing the tattoo on her wrist. "You wanted to talk."

I nod, suddenly unsure where to start. "Yeah, I... Thanks for agreeing to this. I know it's late, and you probably want to get home to Roman."

She gives me a small smile. "It's okay. He's with my cousin. But yeah, let's talk."

I take a deep breath. "I wanted to apologize again for not coming in earlier. And for showing up at your car like that. It wasn't... I wasn't thinking straight."

Lauren nods, her expression guarded. "You said you almost did something you'd regret. Do you want to talk about that?"

The waitress returns with our coffees, giving me a moment to collect my thoughts. As she walks away, I wrap my hands around the warm mug, anchoring myself.

"I almost drank last night," I admit quietly. "Went as far as buying a bottle. But I couldn't do it. I've worked too hard to throw it all away."

Lauren's eyes soften slightly. She leans forward, her elbows on the table, coffee mug cradled between her hands. The steam rises, momentarily obscuring her face. "That must have been difficult. How long have you been sober?"

I run a hand through my hair, feeling the grease and grime from the day. A reminder of how close I came to falling apart completely. "Three years," I say, my voice rough. I clear my throat. "Well, until a couple nights ago. I slipped up, but I'm trying to get back on track."

She nods, and I can see her processing this information. Her fingers tap a rhythmless beat on the side of her mug. A nervous habit, maybe. "Can I ask... what made you want to drink?"

I laugh humorlessly, the sound harsh in the quiet diner. A few booths over, an elderly couple looks our way. I lower my voice. "What didn't? The third anniversary of my wife's death, the pressure of the band, the constant temptation..." I gesture vaguely with my hand, nearly knocking over the sugar dispenser. Lauren catches it deftly. Our fingers brush, and I feel a jolt of... some-

60

thing. Connection? Electricity? I pull back quickly. "Sometimes it feels like everything's pushing me towards it."

Lauren looks thoughtful for a moment, then says, "You know, it's been three years for me too."

I raise an eyebrow, surprised by the coincidence. "Three years since...?"

Lauren takes a deep breath, her fingers tightening around her coffee mug. "Since Miles, Roman's father, died while I was pregnant. It was an overdose."

The weight of her words hangs between us. I feel a strange mix of connection and unease. My stomach tightens, a chill running down my spine despite the warmth of the diner. The coincidence is too stark, too precise. Three years ago. An overdose. Just like Chloe. It's as if the universe is playing some cruel joke.

"I'm so sorry, Lauren," I manage to say, my voice barely above a whisper. "That must have been incredibly difficult."

She nods, her eyes distant. "It was. Still is, sometimes, especially for Roman. He wasn't even born yet. He never knew his dad at all. And vice versa."

I swallow hard, trying to push down the growing sense of disquiet. "And Chloe... my wife," I say softly, the words feeling heavy on my tongue, "she overdosed too."

Lauren's eyes meet mine, a flash of understanding passing between us. But beneath that, I see a flicker of something else. Confusion? Suspicion? It's gone before I can place it.

"It's a strange coincidence, isn't it?" she says, her voice

carefully neutral. "Both of us losing someone that way, at the same time."

I nod, unsure what to say. The parallels in our stories are striking, but there's something about it that nags at me, a piece that doesn't quite fit. A shadow of doubt creeps into my mind, but I push it aside, not ready to face whatever it might mean.

"I guess we both know something about grief then, too, huh?" I say, trying to lighten the mood slightly.

Lauren gives me a small smile. "Yeah, I guess we do. It's not exactly the kind of common ground you hope for when getting to know someone."

"No," I agree, "but maybe it helps us understand each other a little better."

She nods, and I can see her relaxing slightly. "Maybe it does. And look, you resisted the temptation last night. That's positive."

"Yeah. Barely." I look up at her. "Talking to you... it helped. More than you know."

Lauren looks surprised. "Me? But we barely know each other."

"I know. But you saw me as a person, not just a fucking rockstar or whatever. It's been a long time since anyone's done that."

She's quiet for a moment, stirring her coffee. "Dakota, I... I appreciate your honesty. But I need you to understand something. I have a son. I can't... I can't expose him to..."

"To someone like me," I finish for her.

She winces. "That's not what I meant. It's just... I've

been down this road before. Obviously, it didn't end well."

I nod, understanding and disappointment warring inside me. "I get it. I do. And you're right to be cautious. I'm not... I'm not in the best place right now."

"Then why are you here?" she asks, her voice gentle but firm.

I meet her eyes, trying to convey the sincerity I feel. "Because talking to you makes me want to be better. To do better. I know that's a lot of pressure to put on someone I barely know, and I'm sorry for that. But I just... I felt a connection with you, and I wanted to explore that. If you're willing."

Lauren looks conflicted, and I brace myself for rejection. But then she surprises me.

"Okay," she says slowly, holding out a hand. "Let's start over. Hi, I'm Lauren. I'm a single mom who works too much and worries too much. And you are?"

I can't help but smile, reaching out to shake her hand. "I'm Dakota. Bassist for Chaos Fuel, recovering addict, and guy who's trying to figure out how to be a decent human being."

As we continue talking, I find myself drawn to the way her eyes change with her emotions. When she talks about Roman, they light up with fierce love and pride. But when the conversation turns to Miles, a shadow passes over them, darkening their hazel hue to almost green. It's not just grief I see there, but a strength, a resilience that's both beautiful and intimidating.

She tucks a strand of hair behind her ear, a gesture

that seems unconscious but draws my attention to the graceful curve of her neck. There's a small scar just below her jawline, barely noticeable unless you're looking closely. I find myself wondering about its story, about all the stories etched into her skin and hidden behind her eyes.

But it's more than just physical attraction. It's the way she holds herself, shoulders back, chin up, despite the weight she carries. It's the hint of a dimple when she offers a half-smile, as if she's not quite ready to let herself fully express joy. It's the gentle but firm way she speaks, every word measured and meaningful.

I realize I'm staring and quickly look down at my coffee. But the image of her stays with me, a complex tapestry of strength and vulnerability that I find myself wanting to understand more deeply.

"Sorry," I say, realizing she's waiting for me to respond. "I just... you remind me of someone."

"Oh?" she asks, eyebrow raised.

I shake my head, smiling ruefully. "No, not like that. You remind me of who I want to be, I guess. Someone who's been through hell but still shows up every day, still fights."

A faint blush colors her cheeks, and for a moment, I see her guard lower just a fraction. It's enough to make me want to see more, to be the kind of person she might let in.

"Thank you," she mutters, dropping her eyes to the table to avoid my gaze. "I just do whatever I have to. Like any mother would. I'm not special."

"Wrong," I say a bit too forcefully. "I have a feeling you're very special."

I reach over and grab her fidgeting hand, noticing that my own has stopped trembling for once. She tenses at first but then relaxes into my palm. Her skin is warm and soft against my callouses, and I rub my thumb along her knuckles slowly, savoring the feeling.

As we settle into a more relaxed conversation, sharing stories and laughing over the terrible diner pie, I can't shake the feeling that this—whatever this is—could be the beginning of something important. Something healing for both of us.

I just hope I don't fucking screw it up.

eleven
stay away

Lauren

The night air is cool against my skin as Dakota and I walk back to my car. The streets are quiet, our footsteps echoing in the empty parking lot. I'm hyper-aware of his presence beside me, the slight brush of his arm against mine sending shivers down my spine. I'm half tempted to let our fingers slide together and hold his hand. It would feel completely natural, but I can't quite allow myself to do it. I don't really know what's going on between us yet.

I shouldn't feel this way. I've known this man for only a few days, and already he's stirring up emotions I thought I'd buried long ago. It's dangerous, foolish even. But I can't deny the pull I feel towards him.

Roman's face flashes in my mind, his innocent smile and trusting eyes a stark reminder of my responsibilities. What would he think of his mom getting involved with a rockstar? With an addict, no less? The thought of intro-ducing any instability into his life makes my stomach turn. He's already been through so much, lost so much. More than he even realizes yet.

And then there's the practical side. The early mornings getting him ready for daycare, the late nights soothing his nightmares, the constant juggling of work and motherhood. How could someone like Dakota, with his unpredictable schedule and complex past, possibly fit into that?

But even as these thoughts race through my mind, I can't ignore how my heart speeds up when Dakota's arm brushes against mine. The way his presence makes me feel both excited and at peace, a combination I haven't experienced in years.

"So," Dakota says, breaking the comfortable silence between us. "This is you, right?"

We've reached my car, and I nod, fumbling for my keys. "Yeah, this is me."

I turn to face him, and my breath catches in my throat. The streetlight casts a soft glow on his features, highlighting the sharp line of his jaw and the fullness of his lips. His dark hair is slightly tousled, a few strands falling across his forehead in a way that makes my fingers itch to brush them back.

But the vulnerability I see in his eyes truly takes my breath away. Those deep brown eyes, usually so guarded, now seem to hold a universe of emotion. The contrast between the rockstar I've seen in videos and this raw, open man before me is striking. And if I'm being honest with myself, it's utterly captivating.

It's so different from what I saw in Miles. Where

Miles had bravado and charm that masked his demons, Dakota's struggles are right there on the surface. He's not hiding, not pretending to be something he's not.

"Lauren," he starts, his voice soft. "I want you to know how much tonight meant to me. Talking with you, it's given me hope. Something to hold onto."

His words send a warmth spreading through my chest, but I force myself to remember the reality of our situation. "Dakota, I meant what I said before. I have to be careful. Roman—"

"I know," he interrupts gently. "And I respect that. I'm not asking for anything. I just want you to know that you've inspired me to be better. To try harder."

I search his face, looking for any sign of insincerity, any hint of the manipulation I'd grown so accustomed to with Miles. But all I see is earnestness, determination, and a flicker of something else. Something that makes my heart race.

"I believe you," I say softly, surprised to find that I mean it. "And I've enjoyed talking with you too."

Dakota's face lights up with a smile that makes him look younger, unburdened. Without thinking, I reach out and touch his arm. The contact sends a jolt through me, and I see his eyes widen in response.

"But," I continue, forcing myself to be the voice of reason, "we need to take this slow. Whatever 'this' is. I can't rush into anything, not with Roman to consider."

Dakota nods, his expression serious. "Of course. Slow is good. Slow is... safe."

We stand there for a moment, neither of us quite

ready to say goodbye. I know I should get in my car and drive away, put some distance between us before I do something reckless. But I can't bring myself to move.

"So," Dakota says, a hint of nervousness in his voice. "Can I see you again?"

I hesitate, my mind warring with my heart. Every instinct honed by years of single motherhood and past hurts is screaming at me to say no, to protect myself and Roman from potential pain. But there's another voice, one I haven't heard in a long time, urging me to take a chance.

"Yes," I hear myself say, almost in disbelief. "Yes, I'd like that."

The smile that breaks across Dakota's face is radiant, and I feel an answering smile tugging at my own lips.

"Good," he says softly, leaning down to place a light kiss on my forehead before stepping away. It's so quick and unexpected, I'm not sure how to react. So, I don't. I just blink a few times to try to gather my wits, but it's difficult with his spicy scent still surrounding me.

"Goodnight, Dakota," I finally say, forcing myself to unlock my car and slide into the driver's seat. It's all I could think to do in response to his kiss. What does someone do when a guy does that? Obviously, jump in your car and drive away as soon as possible, right?

He smiles and waves as he walks backward to his own car. And all the while, I can't shake the feeling that I'm standing on the edge of something momentous.

I just hope I'm strong enough to handle whatever the hell it is.

twelve
remember me

Dakota

The city lights blur past my window as I navigate the late-night streets of LA. My hands are steady on the wheel, steadier than they've been in days. The tremors that have haunted me since my slip-up are gone, replaced by a strange calm.

Lauren's scent still lingers on my clothes, a mix of coffee and something uniquely her. I can still feel the softness of her skin where I kissed her forehead, can still see the surprise in her eyes at the gesture. Maybe I overstepped. But God, it felt right.

I turn up the radio, trying to drown out the voice in my head that's screaming at me to turn around, to go back to her. It's too soon. We both know it. But knowing doesn't make it any easier.

At a red light, I find myself reaching for my phone. I want to text her, to make sure she got home safe, to hear her voice one more time. But I stop myself. Slow, I remind myself. We agreed on slow.

The light turns green, and I accelerate, feeling the power of the car beneath me. It's nothing compared to the rush I felt talking to Lauren, though. And that scares the shit out of me.

I've been down this road before. Falling fast, thinking someone could save me from myself. But Lauren... she's different. She's not trying to save me. She's inspiring me to save myself.

As I pull into my driveway, I realize I've driven the whole way without once thinking about drinking. Without that gnawing need clawing at my insides. It's been so long since that happened, I almost don't recognize the feeling.

Is this what hope feels like?

I kill the engine and sit in the darkness for a moment, letting the events of the night wash over me. The pain of almost slipping, the fear of disappointing the band, the unexpected connection with Lauren. It's all swirling in my head, a cocktail of emotions I'm not sure how to process.

But one thing is clear as I finally drag myself out of the car and towards my front door: something has shifted. Something fundamental.

For the first time in three years, I'm looking forward to tomorrow. And it's not because of a show, or a recording session, or anything to do with the band.

It's because of her. Because of Lauren.

As I fumble with my keys, a realization hits me like a ton of bricks: I'm in trouble. Deep, life-changing trouble.

And the scariest part? I think I might be okay with that.

I push open the front door, the silence of the house a stark contrast to the chaotic thoughts in my head. But as I step into the living room, I realize it's not as empty as I expected.

Connor, my roommate, is sprawled on the couch, an empty bottle of Angel's Envy on the coffee table in front of him. My stomach drops as I recognize it—the same bottle I bought last night in my moment of weakness.

"Hey, man," Connor slurs, lifting his head. "You're home late."

I stand frozen, staring at the empty bottle. The bottle that was supposed to be my downfall. The bottle I resisted. "Connor, what the fuck?"

He follows my gaze and has the decency to look sheepish. "Oh, that. I found it in your room when I was looking for a phone charger. Figured I'd help you out, you know? Can't drink it if it's gone, right?"

His words hit me like a truck. Is that what it looks like from the outside? Your friend finding your hidden stash and thinking the only way to help is to remove the temptation?

"You shouldn't have done that," I say, my voice low and controlled despite the anger and shame bubbling up inside me.

Connor sits up, swaying slightly. "Come on, Dakota. We both know you're not supposed to have that stuff around. I was just looking out for you."

I close my eyes, taking a deep breath. When I open

them, I see Connor through new eyes. The worry lines on his forehead, the cautious way he's watching me, like I might explode at any moment. Is this how everyone sees me? A ticking time bomb of addiction?

"I appreciate the thought," I say finally, "but next time, just talk to me, okay? Don't go through my stuff, and definitely don't drink yourself into a stupor on my account."

Connor nods, looking properly chastised. "Sorry, man. I just... I worry about you, you know?"

The anger drains out of me, replaced by a weariness that settles deep in my bones. "I know. But I'm working on it. I'm trying to be better."

As I help Connor to his feet and guide him to his room, Lauren's face flashes in my mind. Her belief in me, her cautious hope. I want to be the person she sees when she looks at me, not this fragile addict that everyone else seems to see.

Back in my own room, I sink onto the bed, the events of the night crashing over me. The near-miss with drinking, the unexpected connection with Lauren, and now this sobering reminder of how far I still have to go.

My body feels heavy, like I've just played a three-hour set. Every muscle aches, tension coiled tight in my shoulders and neck. I run a hand over my face, feeling the stubble that's grown throughout the day, rough against my palm. My eyes burn with exhaustion, and there's a dull throbbing at my temples - the precursor to what will likely be a killer headache.

But despite the physical toll, there's something else there, too. A strange lightness in my chest, as if a weight I've been carrying for years has started to lift. It's an unfamiliar feeling, this mixture of bone-deep weariness and... hope?

As I lay there in the darkness, I realize something. For the first time in years, I'm not reaching for a bottle to numb these feelings. I'm sitting with them, uncomfortable as they are.

Maybe that's what real progress looks like.

I lay in bed, staring at the ceiling, allowing the emotions I usually avoid to wash over me. It's uncomfortable, like an ill-fitting suit, but I force myself to sit with it.

First, there's the shame. Shame that Connor felt he needed to "save" me from myself. Shame that I bought that bottle in the first place. It's a familiar feeling, one that's been my constant companion for years. But now, instead of drowning it in alcohol, I let it exist. I acknowledge it. This shame is part of me, but it doesn't define me.

Then there's the fear. Fear of falling off the wagon for real next time. Fear of disappointing the band, my fans, myself. And now, fear of disappointing Lauren. It's a paralyzing feeling, but I breathe through it. Fear means I care. It means I have something to lose, something to fight for.

Anger bubbles up next. Anger at myself for being weak, at Connor for overstepping, at the world for making sobriety so damn hard. I clench and unclench my fists, letting the anger flow through me without acting on it. It's okay to be angry, I remind myself. It's what I do with that anger that matters.

And underneath it all, there's a current of grief. Grief for Chloe, for the life we could have had. It's been three years, but the pain is still there, a dull ache in my chest. I let myself feel it fully for the first time in a long time. Tears prick at my eyes, and I let them fall. It's okay to miss her, to mourn what could have been.

If I'm honest with myself, I've been slowly and silently drowning in this grief every fucking day. Missing what we had. Missing what we could have had. Just an entire piece of me – missing. It's no way to fucking live.

Not anymore.

But then I get really honest. In my grief, I've only mourned the good times. In truth, they weren't all good. Both of us struggled with our sobriety, and sometimes, it was downright ugly. But the heart doesn't want to remember that shit. It only wants to focus on the good that we've lost. Not the bad. Why the fuck does my brain work that way? Turning Chloe into some sort of saint because she's dead?

Because she loved me. And I loved her. And that was all that mattered in the end.

The end... how fucking poetic. What good is it now? What was all that love for if it was going to turn out the way it did anyway? Am I even grieving a person anymore? Or just my memory of her? Is there a fucking difference?

Is there a right way to grieve? A socially correct way? A time limit? What does 'letting go' even feel like? What am I letting go of? My loyalty? My love? Or is it just my obsession with my loss?

Whatever it is, I can feel that tether thinning. My white-knuckled grasp on it is loosening. It hurts like fucking hell, but I can't go on like this.

I need to let Chloe go.

As I lay there, feeling everything, a new thought surfaces. The matching three-year anniversary. Lauren's loss mirroring my own. It still bothers me. An itch at the back of my mind that I can't quite scratch. It's too neat, too coincidental. But I push that thought aside for now. That's a mystery for another day.

For now, I focus on breathing. In and out. Feeling each emotion as it comes, acknowledging it, and letting it pass. It's exhausting, but also... freeing. Like I'm finally facing the demons I've been running from for so long.

I realize that this - sitting with my feelings, processing them without numbing them - this is how I can deal with them now. It's not easy, and it's not pleasant, but it's real. It's growth.

As the first light of dawn starts to peek through my curtains, I feel drained but oddly at peace. I've made it through the night without a drink, faced my emotions head-on, and come out the other side.

Maybe this is what Lauren sees in me. Not just the mess, but the potential. The strength to face my demons and keep going.

With that thought, I finally drift off to sleep, feeling

more like myself than I have in years. Tomorrow is a new day, and for the first time in a long time, I feel ready to face it.

thirteen
drive

Lauren

The dinner rush is in full swing, and I'm juggling plates and orders with practiced ease. But even as I smile at customers and refill coffee cups, a part of my mind is elsewhere. With him.

Dakota.

Every time the bell above the door jingles, my heart does a little flip. I find myself scanning the incoming customers, half-expecting to see his tall frame and messy dark hair. But as the night wears on, there's no sign of him.

"Order up for table six!" Jen's voice cuts through my thoughts.

I grab the plates, forcing myself to focus. What am I doing? We never even exchanged numbers. He said he wanted to see me again, but maybe he changed his mind. If he'd really wanted to see me again, wouldn't he have gotten my number? Maybe the light of day made him realize how complicated this could get. It's not as if I'm a great catch being a poor single mom. I know this.

But then again, a small voice in my head argues, maybe he's respecting your boundaries. You did say you needed to take things slow. And isn't showing up in person more meaningful than a text? It takes more effort, more courage.

I shake my head, trying to clear these conflicting thoughts. Maybe he's just as nervous and unsure as I am. God knows I've been second-guessing myself all day.

The truth is, I have no idea what he's thinking. And that uncertainty is both thrilling and terrifying.

As I deliver the food to a boisterous family, I can't help but think of Roman. Of how his face lit up this morning when I told him about our upcoming day off together. How can I even consider bringing someone new into our carefully balanced life? Someone like Dakota would definitely upset our norm. But then, with Shannon leaving soon, it's all going to change anyway, right? Why not add another factor to the messed-up equation?

But still, as the night progresses, I can't shake the memory of Dakota's gentle eyes, the warmth of his hand on mine. The way he made me feel seen for the first time in years. Things like that have to mean something, don't they?

Finally, the last customer leaves, and I flip the sign to 'Closed' with a mixture of relief and disappointment. He didn't come. I try to squash the feeling of being let down as I clean up and gather my things.

"Goodnight, Jen," I call as I head out the back door. The cool night air hits my face, and I take a deep breath, trying to clear my head.

And then I see him.

My breath catches in my throat, and for a moment, I'm frozen in place. A wave of heat rushes through me, from my toes to the tips of my ears, followed by a swarm of butterflies taking flight in my stomach. My heart, which had been steadily slowing after the busy shift, suddenly shifts into overdrive.

Dakota is leaning against my car, just like last night. His hands are shoved in his pockets, and he looks up as I approach, nervousness and hope on his face. In the dim light of the parking lot, his eyes seem to glow, drawing me in like a magnet. I have to consciously remind myself to breathe, to put one foot in front of the other as I walk towards him.

My fingers tingle with the memory of his touch, and I have to resist the urge to reach out and make sure he's real, not just a figment of my imagination conjured up by a long day and too much wishful thinking.

"Hi," he says softly.

"Hi," I reply, my heart suddenly racing. "I didn't think you'd come."

He runs a hand through his hair, a gesture I'm starting to recognize as a nervous habit. "I wasn't sure if I should. But I couldn't stop thinking about you all day."

The admission sends a warm flutter through my chest. "Me too," I confess before I can stop myself.

A smile breaks across his face, and God, it's beautiful. "Yeah?"

I nod, unable to keep the answering smile off my face. "Yeah."

We stand there for a moment, just looking at each other. There's so much I want to say, so many questions I want to ask. But for now, this feels like enough. This quiet moment of connection in the dim light of the parking lot.

A small voice in the back of my mind reminds me of the practicalities. How would this work? My life revolves around early mornings with Roman, long shifts at the diner, and stolen moments of rest in between. Dakota's world of late-night gigs, recording sessions, and unpredictable schedules seems so far removed from mine.

I think about Jen's knowing looks when I've been distracted all day, about how I'll need to be even more focused to avoid mistakes at work. About the possibility of Dakota showing up during my shifts, and how that might affect my job performance. Would my boss understand if I got flustered because a rockstar was sitting in my section?

And what about Roman's routine? His stability is everything to me. How would I balance bedtime stories and Dakota's evening shows? Parent-teacher conferences and backstage passes?

The questions swirl in my mind, a dizzying array of 'what ifs' and 'how coulds.' But as I look at Dakota, feeling the warmth of his presence, I realize that, for once, I want to push those practical concerns aside. Just for a moment, I want to exist in this bubble where anything seems possible.

"So," Dakota says finally, "do you maybe want to grab a coffee again or something? If you're not too tired, I mean."

I glance at my watch, a reflex born from years of juggling responsibilities. It's later than I thought, and I know Shannon is probably waiting up for me. She's been packing for her move to Seattle, and we were supposed to go over some logistics for her departure. Roman should be asleep by now, but what if he wakes up and I'm not there?

The responsible part of me, the part that's always aware of time ticking away and obligations to be met, urges me to decline. To thank Dakota for coming, but to head home where I'm needed. Shannon's leaving soon, and every moment with her feels precious now.

But another part of me, a part I thought had long since gone dormant, rebels against the constant tug of responsibility. *Just this once*, it whispers, *just for a little while, can't you do something for yourself?*

I look back at Dakota, seeing the hope in his eyes, and I make a decision.

I know I should say no. I should go home to Roman, stick to my routine, and play it safe. But as I look into Dakota's eyes, I find myself nodding.

"I'd like that," I say.

As we walk towards the all-night diner down the street, our hands brushing together and our fingers eventually entwining, I can't help but feel that maybe, just maybe, this is the start of something beautiful.

And terrifying.

But mostly beautiful.

We settle into a booth at the all-night diner, the same one we were in just last night. It feels familiar and strange, like we're picking up a conversation we never finished.

"So," Dakota says, wrapping his hands around his coffee mug. "Tell me more about Miles. If you're comfortable with that, I mean."

I take a deep breath, stirring my tea absently. "It's... complicated," I start, then laugh humorlessly. "But I guess that's true for most relationships, right?"

Dakota nods, his eyes encouraging me to continue.

"Miles and I, we weren't... we weren't in a good place when he died," I admit, the words feeling heavy on my tongue. "We fought a lot. About his drug use, his drinking, about money, about the baby... about everything, really."

I see a flicker of surprise in Dakota's eyes. "I'm sorry," he says softly. "That must have been hard."

I nod, swallowing past the lump in my throat. "The thing is, I was angry with him for so long. Even after he died, I was angry. And then I felt guilty for being angry because you're not supposed to speak ill of the dead, right?"

Dakota reaches across the table, his hand covering

mine. The warmth of his touch is comforting. "There's no right or wrong way to grieve, Lauren."

His words unlock something in me, and suddenly, I'm talking more than I have in years. "I loved Miles, I did. But towards the end, I think I loved the idea of who he could be more than who he actually was. And then he died, and I was left with all these unresolved feelings and a baby on the way."

I look up at Dakota, suddenly aware of how different our situations are. "I'm sorry. I shouldn't be dumping all this on you. Your loss... it's different."

Dakota squeezes my hand gently. "Different, yeah. But pain is pain, Lauren. Your feelings are valid."

He's quiet for a moment, his eyes distant. "Chloe and I, we were happy. At least, I thought we were. Her death... it blindsided me. One day, we were planning our future, and the next..."

He trails off, and I can see the raw pain in his eyes. I turn my hand over, intertwining our fingers. "I'm so sorry, Dakota."

He gives me a sad smile. "Sometimes I think it might have been easier if we had been fighting. If there had been signs. I mean, things weren't perfect. They never are. But it was so sudden, so final. I didn't get to say goodbye, didn't get to tell her one last time that I loved her."

We sit in silence for a moment, both lost in our memories. Despite the differences in our experiences, there's a shared understanding between us. A recognition of the pain, the guilt, the what-ifs that come with loss.

"You know," I say finally, "I think in some ways, you're braver than I am."

Dakota looks at me, confused. "What do you mean?"

"You loved Chloe wholly, without reservation. Even now, you honor that love," I explain. "I've been so scared to love like that again. Scared to be hurt, scared to lose someone else."

Dakota's thumb traces circles on the back of my hand. "I don't know if it's bravery," he says softly. "Sometimes it feels more like a curse. To have known that kind of love and lost it."

I nod, understanding. "But you're here," I say, gesturing between us. "You're trying. That's brave."

He smiles, a real smile that reaches his eyes. "So are you, Lauren. So are you."

After a comfortable pause, Dakota leans back, his fingers still intertwined with mine. "So, enough about the heavy stuff for now. Tell me something good, something you're looking forward to or dreaming about."

I hesitate for a moment, then decide to share. "Well, I've been thinking about going back to school. Nursing, actually."

Dakota's eyes light up. "Really? That's awesome, Lauren. What made you choose nursing?"

I can't help but smile at his enthusiasm. "I've always wanted to help people. And after everything with Miles, and then taking care of Roman... I don't know. It just feels right. I'm a caretaker by nature, I think. Like I could make a real difference, you know?"

He nods, understanding in his eyes. "I get that. It's

like with music for me. When I'm playing, when I see how our songs affect people, it feels like I'm doing something meaningful."

"Speaking of music," I say, genuinely curious, "how's everything going with the band? You mentioned you guys are getting ready for a tour?"

Dakota's face lights up, and I can see the passion he has for his work. "Yeah, we're in the final stages of prep. It's exciting but also a little terrifying. We're playing bigger venues this time, more press coverage. It's a whole new level for us."

"That sounds amazing," I say, trying to imagine what that kind of life must be like. "How do you balance it all? The touring, the recording, the public attention?"

He laughs, running a hand through his hair. "Honestly? Sometimes, I'm not sure I do balance it. It's a lot of late nights, early mornings, and living out of a suitcase. But when we're on stage, when everything clicks, and the crowd is with us... there's no feeling like it in the world."

I listen, fascinated, as he tells me about life on the road, about the camaraderie with his bandmates, about the thrill of creating music. It's a world so different from mine, and yet I find myself drawn in by his passion.

"You know," I say, a thought occurring to me, "I think there's something similar in what we both want to do. Different scales, maybe, but the core is the same."

Dakota looks intrigued. "What do you mean?"

"Well, as a nurse, I'd be trying to help people, to make their lives better in some way, even if it's just easing their pain for a moment," I explain. "And isn't that what you do with your music? You connect with people, you make them feel something, maybe help them through tough times or celebrate good ones."

His eyes widen slightly, and a slow smile spreads across his face. "I never thought about it like that, but you're right. It's all about human connection, isn't it?"

I nod, feeling a surge of warmth at his understanding. "Exactly. Different methods, same goal."

As we continue chatting, jumping from topic to topic with an ease that surprises me, I realize how much we actually have in common despite our different worlds. We both value connection - whether it's with an audience or with patients. We both want to make a difference in people's lives. And we both know what it's like to have a passion that drives us.

The conversation flows naturally, punctuated by laughter and moments of shared understanding. And with each passing minute, I feel the connection between us growing stronger, more real.

It's scary and exhilarating all at once. But for the first time in years, I find myself excited about the possibilities the future might hold.

fourteen
power over me

Dakota

As Lauren and I step out of the diner, the night air hits us, cool and crisp. The neon sign above the diner flickers, casting an intermittent red glow over the cracked sidewalk. In the distance, I can hear the faint wail of a siren, a reminder of the city that never truly sleeps.

Our hands find each other almost instinctively, fingers interlocking as we walk. The streets are surprisingly quiet for LA, with only the occasional car passing by, its headlights briefly illuminating our path before plunging us back into the soft darkness. Overhead, the moon peeks out from behind wispy clouds, a silent observer of our midnight stroll.

As we pass under a streetlight, I catch a glimpse of Lauren's profile - the curve of her cheek, the slight upturn of her lips. My heart pounds in my chest, a steady rhythm of anticipation and nerves that seem to echo off the buildings around us.

We pass a closed storefront, its windows dark and

reflective. For a moment, I see our silhouettes mirrored back at us - two figures, close together, moving in sync. It strikes me how natural this feels, how right, despite the newness of it all.

As we approach Lauren's car, the only one left in the small parking lot besides mine, gravel crunches under our feet. The sound seems amplified in the quiet night, as if the universe is holding its breath, waiting to see what happens next.

"I had a really good time tonight," Lauren says softly, her voice barely above a whisper.

I squeeze her hand gently. "Me too. I'm glad I waited for you."

She looks up at me, a small smile playing on her lips. "I'm glad you did, too."

We reach her car far too quickly for my liking. Lauren leans against the driver's side door, her eyes meeting mine. In the dim light of the streetlamp, she looks beautiful - tired, yes, but with a spark in her eyes that wasn't there earlier.

"So," I say, suddenly feeling like a teenager on his first date. "I guess this is goodnight."

Lauren nods, but doesn't move to get in her car. "I guess it is."

There's a moment of charged silence between us. I can feel the pull towards her, like gravity. My eyes flick down to her lips, then back up to her eyes. I see the same want reflected there, mixed with a hint of hesitation.

"Lauren," I breathe, stepping closer. "I really want to kiss you right now."

She swallows hard, her fingers tightening around mine. "I would love that."

That's all the invitation I need. I lean in slowly, giving her time to pull away if she changes her mind. But she doesn't. Instead, she tilts her face up to mine.

Our lips meet, and it's like a jolt of electricity through my body. Her lips are soft, warm, and she tastes faintly of the tea she had at the diner. I bring my free hand up to cup her cheek, deepening the kiss. Every nerve ending in my body seems to come alive. I'm hyper-aware of every point of contact between us - her hand on my chest, my fingers tangled in her hair, the slight pressure of her body against mine.

As the kiss intensifies, I feel a warmth spreading from my core to my fingertips. My heart is pounding so hard I'm sure Lauren must feel it. The world around us fades away, and all I can focus on is the softness of her lips, the gentle caress of her breath on my skin, and the intoxicating scent that's uniquely her.

When we finally pull apart, I feel dizzy, like I've just come off stage after an intense performance. My lips tingle, already missing her touch. I can still feel the ghost of her kiss, the impression of her body against mine. It's been so long since I've felt this alive, this present in my own skin.

"Wow," she says softly, a shy smile on her face.

I can't help but grin. "Yeah. Wow."

I close my eyes for a moment, savoring the sensation. When I open them, I'm met with Lauren's gaze, her hazel eyes wide and bright. There's a softness there that wasn't present earlier in the evening, a vulnerability that makes my heart ache in the best possible way.

Lauren's hand, which had been resting on my chest, slowly slides up to the nape of my neck. Her fingers thread through my hair, sending a shiver down my spine. I watch as she bites her lower lip, a gesture I'm quickly learning means she's deep in thought.

"Dakota," she whispers, her voice slightly husky. She clears her throat and tries again. "Dakota, I... this is..."

I can see the conflict playing out on her face - the desire, the hesitation, the hope, and the fear all warring for dominance. Her eyes flick down to my lips and then back up, and I feel her lean in almost imperceptibly.

But then she takes a small step back, her hand falling from my neck to rest on my arm. She doesn't let go completely, though, her grip tightening slightly as if she's anchoring herself.

"This is nice," she finally says, a small, hesitant smile tugging at her lips. "Really nice. But also..."

"Scary?" I offer, and I see relief flood her features.

"Yeah," she nods, letting out a breath. "Scary."

I watch as she squares her shoulders, a determined look settling over her face. It's the same look I saw when she talked about going back to school, about making a difference. It makes me want to know every facet of her, to understand all the layers that make up Lauren.

"But maybe," she continues, her voice stronger now, "maybe scary isn't always bad?"

The hope in her voice, the tentative optimism in her eyes - it's almost too much. I want to pull her close again, to promise her the world. Instead, I settle for bringing her hand to my lips and placing a gentle kiss on her knuckles.

"No," I agree, my voice rough with emotion. "Sometimes scary can be pretty damn amazing."

The smile that breaks across her face is radiant, lighting up the entire parking lot. As she leans in for another kiss, I can feel her smile against my lips, and can sense the mix of excitement and nervousness in the way her body trembles slightly against mine.

At this moment, I'm acutely aware of every little reaction, every small gesture. And I know, without a doubt, that I'm not alone in falling hard and fast.

We break the kiss, my forehead resting against Lauren's, and a realization hits me. For the first time in what feels like forever, I haven't thought about drinking all evening. The usual gnawing need, the constant battle against cravings - it's all been quiet.

I take a deep breath, inhaling her scent, and it dawns on me that she's become a different kind of intoxication. Her presence, her smile, the way she sees me - it's all more potent than any alcohol I've ever tasted.

"You okay?" Lauren asks, noticing my sudden thoughtfulness.

I pull back slightly, meeting her concerned gaze. "Yeah, I'm... I'm great, actually. I just realized something."

"What's that?" she asks, her hand still resting on my chest.

I hesitate for a moment, not wanting to burden her

with the weight of my addiction. But her eyes are open, patient, and I find myself wanting to share this moment with her.

"Being with you... it's the first time in a long time that I haven't felt the need to drink. You make me forget about all that. In a good way."

Lauren's eyes widen slightly, and I see a mix of emotions flash across her face - surprise, concern, and something that looks a lot like hope.

"Dakota," she says softly, "that's... I'm glad. But I don't want you to feel like you have to rely on me for that. Your sobriety is your journey."

Her words, gentle but firm, remind me why I'm drawn to her. She doesn't try to fix me or take on my battles. She just... sees me.

"I know," I assure her. "And I'm not putting that on you. I just... I wanted you to know that you have a positive effect on me. More than you realize."

We stand there for a moment, neither of us wanting to break the spell. But reality starts to creep back in, and I see Lauren glance at her watch.

"I should go," she says reluctantly. "Roman..."

I nod, understanding. "Of course. Can I see you again soon?"

Lauren smiles, and it's like the sun coming out. "I'd like that."

As I watch Lauren input her number into my phone, a thought hits me like a freight train. The tour. It's looming on the horizon, just weeks away. The excitement

I've felt about it suddenly mixes with a new kind of anxiety.

"Lauren," I start, my voice hesitant. She looks up, her eyes questioning. "I should probably tell you. The band, we're going on tour soon. For a few months."

I see a flicker of something - disappointment? Concern? - cross her face before she schools her features into a neutral expression. "Oh," she says softly. "When do you leave?"

"A few weeks," I reply, hating how final it sounds. "I don't want this to end before it's even had a chance to start."

Lauren's quiet for a moment, and I can almost see the gears turning in her head. "It doesn't have to," she says finally. "I mean, if you don't want it to. We'll see where this goes in the next few weeks. And then, well, there's always phone calls and FaceTime, right?"

Her attempt at optimism warms my heart, but I can't help but think of the realities of tour life. The late nights, the constant travel, the temptations... And Lauren has Roman to think about. How fair would it be to ask her to wait around for me?

"Yeah," I say, trying to match her tone. "We'll figure it out."

But as I lean in for another kiss, I can't shake the feeling that we're on borrowed time. The road has always been my home, my escape. Now, for the first time, I'm not sure I want to leave.

I push the thought aside, determined to live in this

moment. But I know it's a conversation we'll need to have sooner rather than later. For now, though, I just want to savor this - the feel of Lauren in my arms, the promise of something new and beautiful, even if it might be fleeting.

As I watch Lauren drive away, a wave of conflicting emotions washes over me. The euphoria of the kiss is still coursing through my veins, but it's tinged with a familiar fear that creeps in at the edges.

I haven't felt this way since Chloe. The rush, the excitement, the potential for something real and beautiful. But with that comes the memory of loss, the pain that nearly destroyed me when she died. Am I ready to open myself up to that possibility again?

Lauren is different from Chloe in so many ways, yet there's a similar warmth, a kindness that draws me in. But where my relationship with Chloe felt like a whirlwind romance from the start, this thing with Lauren feels more grounded, more real somehow. Maybe it's because we've both been through so much, or maybe it's just the wisdom that comes with age and experience.

Part of me wants to run, to protect myself from the potential heartbreak. It would be easier to lose myself in the music, in the tour, in the familiar routines of the band.

Safer.

But another part of me, a part that's been dormant for too long, wants to dive in headfirst. To see where this could go, to allow myself to feel deeply again, even if it means risking pain.

As I stand here in the empty parking lot, the ghost of

Lauren's kiss still on my lips, I realize I'm at a crossroads. The path of safety, of emotional distance, lies one way. The path of vulnerability, of potential joy and pain, lies the other.

And for the first time in years, I find myself wanting to take the risk.

I just hope I don't fucking screw this up.

I step into the apartment, the familiar scent of Connor's attempts at cooking filling the air. My roommate's head pops out from the kitchen, a grin on his face.

"Hey man, you're home late. I made... well, I'm not sure what I made, but it's edible. Want some?"

I chuckle, shaking my head. "Thanks, but I think I'll pass. I grabbed a bite at Sunny's."

Connor's eyebrows shoot up. "The diner? Dude, they closed hours ago."

"Yeah, I know. I was... talking to someone."

Connor's eyes narrow, a smirk playing on his lips. "Talking to someone, huh? Would this someone happen to be a certain waitress you've been mentioning a lot lately?"

I feel a flush creep up my neck. "Her name's Lauren, and yeah. We were just talking."

"Just talking," Connor repeats, his tone teasing. Then his expression softens. "That's great, man. Really. It's good to see you putting yourself out there again."

I nod, grateful for his support. Connor's been with

me through it all - Chloe's death, my struggle with alcohol, and now my sobriety.

"She's... she's something else, Con," I admit, settling onto the couch. "Smart, funny, resilient as hell. She's got a kid, you know? A little boy. And she's applying to nursing school."

Connor whistles, joining me in the living room with his mystery meal. "Sounds like she's got her hands full. You sure you're ready for all that?"

It's a fair question. One I've been asking myself a lot lately.

"I don't know," I say honestly. "But I want to find out. For the first time since Chloe... I want to try."

Connor nods, his expression serious. "And the sobriety thing? You've told her about that, right?"

"I did," I admit. " I want to be upfront about everything."

"Good," Connor says. "You've worked hard to get where you are. She should know that."

I'm quiet for a moment, thinking about how far I've come. "Sometimes I can hardly believe it myself. Potentially dating again... it's a lot."

Connor reaches over to clap me on the shoulder. "You've got this, man. And you know I've got your back, right? Whatever you do."

"I know," I say, grateful for his unwavering support. "Thanks, man."

"So," Connor says, a mischievous glint in his eye. "When are you gonna ask her out? For real, I mean. Not just late-night diner talks."

I run a hand through my hair, suddenly nervous. "I don't know. Soon, I hope. If she's interested."

Connor snorts. "Dude, she stayed hours after her shift to talk to you. I'd say she's interested."

I can't help but smile at that. "Maybe you're right."

"Of course I'm right," Connor says, taking a bite of his creation and immediately grimacing. "About Lauren, at least. Definitely not about my cooking skills."

As we laugh and Connor dramatically throws his meal in the trash, I find my mind drifting back to Lauren. To her laugh, her resilience, the way her eyes light up when she talks about her son.

For the first time in a long time, I feel a spark of excitement for the future. A future that, just maybe, could include Lauren.

It's terrifying. It's exhilarating. And I can't wait to see where it leads.

fifteen
dear prudence

Lauren

T he scent of freshly mowed grass mingles with the acrid smell of exhaust as I help Roman out of our beat-up Corolla. The community college looms before us, a maze of brick and possibility. My palms are sweaty as I grip Roman's tiny hand.

"Ready for an adventure, little man?" I ask, forcing cheer into my voice.

Roman nods, his mop of curls bouncing. "Is this where you become a super-nurse, Mommy?"

I can't help but smile. "That's the plan. Though I don't know about the 'super' part."

As we slowly climb the steps, my mind races. I'm excited, terrified, and everything in between. This is my chance to build a better life for us, but the timing couldn't be worse. Shannon's boxes are already half-packed, and Dakota... God, I can still taste his kiss, feel the promise of it. But soon, he'll be gone, too.

The lobby bustles with activity. Students chat

animatedly, their laughter a stark contrast to the knot in my stomach. They hurry past, their backpacks loaded with books and dreams. I wonder if I look as out of place as I feel, a young mom with a toddler in tow. Roman presses against my leg, overwhelmed by the noise and movement.

"It's okay, baby," I murmur, running my fingers through his hair. "Want a lift?"

He nods, and I scoop him up, his familiar weight anchoring me. We make our way to the admissions office, my eyes darting to the posters lining the walls. "RN to BSN Program," one proclaims. "Fast-Track LPN Certification," says another. So many options, so many decisions.

"Mommy?" Roman's voice pulls me back. "Are you scared?"

Leave it to my perceptive little guy to see right through me. "A little," I admit. "But that's okay. Sometimes, the best things in life are a little scary at first."

Like falling for a recovering addict rockstar, a voice in my head adds. I push the thought away.

"Can I help you?" A middle-aged woman with kind eyes smiles at us from behind the counter.

I take a deep breath, feeling the weight of this moment. It's not just about me anymore. It's about Roman, about the life I want to give him. About proving to myself that I can do this, even with my support system crumbling around me.

"Yes," I say, my voice stronger than I feel. "I'm here to

enroll in the nursing program. I was hoping to discuss my options and the application process."

As the woman nods and begins pulling out forms, I feel a mixture of terror and exhilaration. This is it. The first step towards our future, whatever it may hold.

"What specific nursing path are you interested in?" she asks, her pen poised over a notepad.

I take a deep breath, recalling all the research I've done late at night after Roman's gone to bed. "I'm interested in becoming a Registered Nurse," I say, surprised by the steadiness in my voice. "I was hoping you could tell me more about the accelerated ADN program."

The woman smiles encouragingly. "Of course. Our Associate Degree in Nursing program is designed for students like you who are just starting their nursing education. Depending on your scheduling, it typically takes about two to three years of study to complete." Her eyes shift to Roman on my hip, and I gather she means the longer term for me.

I nod, trying to absorb the information. "And after that, I'd be able to work as an RN?"

"That's right," she confirms. "Once you complete the program and pass the NCLEX-RN exam, you'll be licensed to work as a Registered Nurse."

My mind races through the obstacles ahead. "Can you tell me more about the class schedules? And does the college offer any assistance with childcare for students?"

Her eyes soften as she glances at Roman again. "We have evening and weekend classes to accommodate working students. As for childcare, we have a subsidized daycare program, but there's often a waiting list. I'd recommend applying as soon as possible."

My heart sinks, but I try not to let my disappointment show. With Shannon leaving for Seattle and no family to fall back on, childcare options are looking slim. I'll have to juggle work and classes, and maybe even look for a more flexible job. The thought makes my stomach ache.

"And regarding financial aid," I begin, hating how small my voice sounds, "are there any scholarships or grants for single parents?"

As she starts listing options, my mind spins with calculations. Tuition, books, uniforms, rent that will soon double without Shannon... The numbers are dizzying. But all in all, I think I'll be able to do it. At least, I hope I will.

I feel Roman's head grow heavy on my shoulder. He's falling asleep, oblivious to the weight of this moment. I hold him tighter, reminding myself why I'm here. The road ahead looks daunting, but for him, I'll find a way. I have to. It's just us against the world, and failure isn't an option.

And then there's the question of time - how to juggle classes, studying, work, and being there for Roman.

I picture my typical day: waking up at dawn to get Roman ready, rushing to drop him off at daycare, working a full shift at the diner, picking up Roman, making dinner, bath time, bedtime... Where do classes fit in? When do I study? When do I sleep?

The thought of adding school to this delicate

balancing act makes my chest tight. But then I look down at Roman, peacefully dozing on my shoulder, and I know I have to find a way. Maybe I can study during my breaks at work. Maybe I can find online classes for some subjects. It'll be hard, but it's not impossible. Other single parents have done it. I can, too.

"It's a lot to take in, I know," the woman says gently, probably noticing my overwhelmed expression. "But you seem determined. That's half the battle right there."

I manage a smile, feeling a flicker of hope. "I am determined. This isn't just about me anymore. It's about giving my son a better future, no matter what it takes." I don't know why I'm telling her all this. Maybe it's her kind face. Or maybe I'm just excited for the future for once.

As she hands me a stack of forms, I take a deep breath. This could work. It has to work. I've come too far to back down now. Despite the fear and uncertainty, I feel a surge of excitement. This is the beginning of something new, something challenging, but something that could change our lives forever.

I spread the financial aid forms across the kitchen table, my head swimming with information. Roman's soft snores drift from the living room, where he's napping on the couch. I should be focusing on these forms, but my mind keeps wandering to the mountain of changes looming ahead.

My phone buzzes, cutting through my racing thoughts. It's a text from Dakota:

> DAKOTA: Hey beautiful. The Rooftop Cinema Club downtown is showing Across the Universe tonight. Want to join me for a movie under the stars?

My heart skips a beat. I glance at the paperwork scattered before me, then at Roman sleeping peacefully. I should be responsible. I should stay home, fill out these forms, and plan for our future.

But the thought of escaping for a few hours is tempting. To sit under the stars, to lose myself in music and a story about love and dreams... to be with Dakota.

I bite my lip, torn. I can't go unless I have someone to watch Roman. Shannon might be free, but I can't assume she's available. I quickly type out a message to her:

> ME: Hey, any chance you're free tonight to watch Roman for a few hours?

I hold my breath as I wait for her response. A minute later, my phone buzzes:

> SHANNON: Sure thing! I'm just hanging around the house tonight. What time?

Relief washes over me. I respond:

ME: Around 7? Thanks so much!

Almost immediately, my phone rings. It's Shannon.

"Spill," she says as soon as I answer. "Who's the guy?"

I can hear the mix of excitement and concern in her voice. "It's not... I mean..." I stammer, unsure how to explain Dakota.

"Lauren," Shannon's voice softens. "Is it that musician from the diner? The one you were telling me about?"

I sigh. "Yeah, it's Dakota. He wants to go to a movie at the Rooftop Cinema Club."

There's a pause on the other end. "Are you sure about this? I mean, with everything going on... the nursing school, me moving out soon, and isn't he going on tour?"

Her questions mirror my own doubts. "I know, I know. It's complicated. But... I don't know, Shan. Maybe I deserve one night of not overthinking everything?"

Shannon chuckles softly. "You? Not overthinking? That'll be the day." Her tone grows serious again. "Just be careful, okay? And have fun. You do deserve it."

As I hang up, I feel a mix of gratitude for Shannon's support and anxiety about the decision ahead. I pick up my phone again, staring at Dakota's message. The responsible thing would be to say no. To focus on Roman and school and work. But haven't I been responsible for so long? Don't I deserve one night?

My fingers hover over the keypad. Yes or no. Future or present. Head or heart.

I take a deep breath and start typing.

> ME: A movie under the stars sounds
> amazing. What time?

My heart races as I hit send. Dakota's reply comes almost instantly:

> DAKOTA: Great! Movie starts at 8:30. I
> can pick you up at 7ish?

I glance at the clock. That gives me just enough time to get ready after Shannon gets home.

> ME: Sounds perfect. See you then.

There's a pause before his next message appears:

> DAKOTA: Can't wait. It'll be nice to
> escape for a while, just the two of us.

I feel a flutter in my stomach at his words. Then, another text:

> DAKOTA: Oh, and wear something
> warm. It gets chilly up there at night.

His thoughtfulness makes me smile. I'm about to reply when he sends one more message:

> DAKOTA: And Lauren? Thanks for
> saying yes. I know things are
> complicated right now.

I stare at the screen, touched by his understanding. After a moment, I respond:

> ME: Thanks for asking. I think we both could use a little escape.

As I set my phone down, I feel both excitement and nervousness. This is really happening. A date with Dakota. A night for myself.

I look over at the pile of college paperwork and then at Roman, who is still napping peacefully. For a moment, guilt threatens to overshadow my excitement. But I push it aside. One night. I can have one night.

Can't I?

With a deep breath, I stand up. Time to get ready for a movie under the stars.

sixteen
all you need is love

Dakota

I pull up to Lauren's house, my fingers drumming nervously on the steering wheel. The brick house looms before me despite its small size, ordinary yet somehow intimidating. I've played sold-out stadiums, but this... this feels bigger.

I check my reflection in the rearview mirror, running a hand through my hair. The guy staring back at me looks more vulnerable than I'm used to seeing. Is this what Lauren does to me?

Taking a deep breath that smells of the jasmine blooming nearby, I approach her door. The muffled sounds of laughter and a child's excited chatter filter through. My hand hovers over the doorbell. What am I getting myself into? But the memory of Lauren's smile pushes me forward.

The door swings open, and there she is. Lauren's smile lights up her face, her eyes crinkling at the corners. For a second, I forget how to breathe.

"Hey," she says softly, stepping forward. Before I can respond, she rises on her tiptoes and presses a quick, soft kiss to my lips. It's brief, but it sends electricity through my entire body.

"Hi," I manage, grinning like an idiot. The scent of her perfume, something light and floral, lingers between us.

"Come on in," she says, a slight blush coloring her cheeks. "I'm almost ready."

I step inside, still a bit dazed from the kiss but immediately aware of the curious gazes fixed on me. A young woman with Lauren's eyes but with red hair, who must be Shannon, is sitting on the couch. And there, peeking out from behind Lauren's legs is a pair of big brown eyes.

"Dakota, this is my son, Roman," Lauren says, her voice softening as she looks down at the boy. The love in her eyes is palpable, and I feel a twinge of... something. Admiration? Longing? "And this is my cousin and soon-to-be-former roommate, Shannon."

I crouch down to Roman's eye level, ignoring the twinge in my knee from an old stage injury. "Hey there, buddy. It's nice to meet you."

Roman regards me seriously for a moment, his eyes wise beyond his years. Then, a shy smile breaks across his face. "Mommy says you play guitar," he says quietly.

I can't help but grin. "That's right. Maybe someday I can play for you. Do you like music?"

Roman nods enthusiastically. "I love drums!"

Lauren groans playfully. "Don't give him any ideas. The pots and pans have suffered enough."

As I laugh, I catch Lauren watching our interaction, a soft expression on her face that makes my heart skip.

Standing up, I meet Shannon's appraising look. She rises, extending her hand. "So, you're the famous Dakota," she says, her tone a mix of friendliness and caution. Her grip is firm, challenging. "I've heard a lot about you."

I match her grip, feeling like I'm being sized up. "All good things, I hope."

Shannon's smile is enigmatic. "That remains to be seen, doesn't it?" Her eyes flick to Lauren, then back to me. The protective intent is clear.

Lauren rolls her eyes. "Alright, enough with the interrogation," she says, grabbing her jacket. She kneels down to Roman's level. "You be good for Aunt Shannon, okay? Mommy will be back later."

Roman nods, wrapping his arms around Lauren's neck. As they hug, I'm struck by the depth of love between them. It's beautiful and intimidating all at once. Can I fit into this picture? Do I want to?

As we head out the door, Shannon calls out, "Have her back at a reasonable hour, rockstar. And remember, I know people."

Lauren groans, but I can see the affection behind her exasperation. "Ignore her," she tells me as we walk to my car. "She thinks she's funny."

"Nah, I get it," I say, opening the car door for her. "She cares about you. That's a good thing."

Lauren pauses before getting in, her eyes meeting mine. There's a moment of understanding between us, an acknowledgment of the complexities we're both navigating. She reaches out, squeezing my hand briefly before sliding into the seat.

As I close her door and walk around to the driver's side, I take a deep breath. The night air is cool against my face, grounding me in this moment.

I slide into the driver's seat, stealing another glance at Lauren. She's beautiful, the streetlights casting a soft glow on her face. But it's more than that. There's a strength in her eyes, a determination that draws me in.

"Ready for a night under the stars?" I ask, my voice softer than I intended.

Lauren's smile is a mix of excitement and nervousness that mirrors my own feelings. "Ready as I'll ever be," she says, reaching over to squeeze my hand again.

As we pull away, I glance in the rearview mirror. Roman and Shannon are waving from the window. I wave back, feeling the weight of their gazes. This night suddenly feels like much more than just a date. It feels like the start of something big, something that could change everything.

And as I look over at Lauren, bathed in the soft glow of the dashboard lights, I realize I'm okay with that. More than okay.

The elevator dings as we reach the Rooftop Cinema Club, and I feel Lauren's hand tighten in mine. As the doors slide open, the cool night air rushes in, carrying the scent of popcorn and the city below.

Lauren's soft gasp of wonder makes me smile. The Los Angeles skyline stretches out before us, a glittering tapestry of lights against the indigo sky. The rooftop has been transformed into an outdoor cinema, with rows of chairs and loveseats facing a large screen. String lights crisscross overhead, casting a warm glow over everything.

"This is incredible," Lauren breathes, her eyes wide as she takes it all in. "I've lived here for years, and I've never seen the city like this."

I can't help but grin at her reaction. "Come on," I say, gently tugging her hand. "I got us a spot in the back."

We weave through the crowd, the buzz of excited conversation and the faint strains of Beatles music surrounding us. I lead Lauren to an Adirondack loveseat nestled in the back corner, offering a perfect view of both the screen and the city beyond.

"Is this okay?" I ask, suddenly nervous. "We can move closer if you want."

But Lauren's smile puts my fears to rest. "It's perfect," she says, settling into the seat. "I feel like we're in our own little world up here."

I sit beside her, acutely aware of how close we are. Our thighs touch, and I can feel the warmth of her body next to mine. I reach behind the seat and pull out a thick blanket.

"Thought we might need this," I say, draping it over our laps. "It can get chilly up here."

Lauren snuggles into the blanket, her shoulder pressing against mine. "Always prepared, aren't you?" she teases. "Let me guess, you were a Boy Scout?"

I chuckle, feeling some of my nervousness dissipate. "Hardly. More like I've had my share of uncomfortable outdoor gigs. You learn to be prepared."

As we wait for the movie to start, I can't help but steal glances at Lauren. The city lights reflect in her eyes, and the gentle breeze plays with her hair. She looks relaxed, happy. It's a good look on her.

"So," I start, wanting to hear her voice again. "Have you seen this movie before? *Across the Universe*?"

Lauren shakes her head. "No, but I've heard good things. You?"

"I've seen it a couple of times," I admit. "The music... it's incredible. I think you'll like it."

She turns to me, a curious look in her eyes. "Is that why you chose this movie? The music?"

I feel a blush creep up my neck. "Partly," I confess. "But also... I don't know. It's a story about love and dreams and finding yourself. It felt... right."

Lauren's expression softens. She reaches out, her fingers intertwining with mine under the blanket. "It does feel right," she says softly.

The lights dim, and a hush falls over the crowd as the opening notes of "*Girl*" start to play. As the story unfolds on screen, I find my attention split. Half on the movie, half on the woman beside me.

When "*With a Little Help from My Friends*" plays, Lauren leans in close. "This reminds me of Shannon," she whispers. "She's always been there for me."

I nod, understanding. "It's good to have people like

that," I say, thinking of my bandmates and Connor. "People who have your back, no matter what."

As the movie progresses, I feel Lauren lean into me more. Whether it's because of the cooling night air or something else, I'm not sure. But I'm not complaining.

During *"Come Together,"* I notice Lauren tense slightly. On screen, the characters are dealing with the draft and the turmoil of the 60s. I squeeze her hand gently, and she squeezes back.

"You okay?" I whisper.

She nods, but I can see a hint of worry in her eyes. "Just thinking about the future," she murmurs. "Everything's changing so fast."

I feel a pang in my chest, knowing I'm part of that change. The tour looms in my mind, a bittersweet reminder of the complications in our budding relationship.

"Change can be good," I say softly, trying to convince myself as much as her. "It opens up new possibilities."

Lauren looks at me, her eyes searching mine. For a moment, I'm afraid I've said the wrong thing. But then she smiles, a small, hopeful smile that makes my heart race.

"You're right," she says, snuggling closer. "New possibilities."

As *"All You Need Is Love"* fills the air from the movie speakers around us, I wrap my arm around Lauren's shoulders. She fits perfectly against my side, as if she was always meant to be there.

At that moment, under the stars with the city spread out before us and Beatles music permeating the space, I realize I'm exactly where I want to be. Whatever challenges lie ahead, whatever complications we might face, this feels right.

And for the first time in a long time, I don't think about Chloe.

seventeen
miss independent

Lauren

The final notes of "*All You Need Is Love*" fade away, and I find myself blinking back tears. I'm not usually this emotional, but something about the movie, the night, and Dakota's warm presence beside me has left me raw and open.

"That was..." I start, struggling to find the right words.

"Yeah," Dakota agrees, his voice soft and understanding. He stands, offering me his hand. "Come on, I know a great little cafe nearby. We can grab a coffee, maybe talk?"

I take his hand, savoring the warmth of his skin against mine. As we make our way through the dispersing crowd, I'm acutely aware of Dakota's hand on the small of my back, guiding me. It's a simple gesture, but it feels intimate, protective. When was the last time someone took care of me like this?

We step out onto the street, the cool night air nipping at my skin, a stark contrast to the warmth of the blanket we'd been sharing. The city is alive around us, pulsing with energy even at this late hour. The scent of street food mingles with exhaust fumes and the crisp night air.

"It's this way," Dakota says, nodding down the street. "It's about a ten-minute walk. Is that okay?"

I smile, squeezing his hand. "It's perfect. I could use a walk to clear my head a bit."

As we stroll down the sidewalk, our joined hands swinging gently between us, I'm struck by how natural this feels. "You know," I say, breaking the comfortable silence, "I haven't done anything like this in years. Not since before Roman was born."

Dakota's thumb strokes the back of my hand. "It must be hard, balancing everything."

I nod, feeling a familiar pang of guilt. "It is. But Roman... he's worth it. He's my whole world." I pause, then add softly, "But sometimes I wonder if I'm enough for him."

Dakota stops, turning to face me. His eyes are intense, sincere. "Lauren, from what I've seen and heard, you're an amazing mother. Roman is lucky to have you."

His words warm me from the inside out, but a nagging doubt persists. How can he know that after such a short time? And what happens when he realizes how complicated my life really is?

Before I can voice these thoughts, Dakota pulls me close. His eyes search mine for a moment, and I see a mixture of desire and uncertainty there. "Lauren," he breathes, and the way he says my name sends shivers down my spine.

I rise up on my tiptoes, meeting him halfway. Our lips meet, and the world falls away.

This kiss is different from our first. That one was sweet, and tentative. This... this is heat and passion and longing. Dakota's hands cup my face, his thumbs stroking my cheeks as his lips move against mine. I taste mint and a hint of sweetness, and feel the slight scratch of his stubble against my skin. I wrap my arms around his neck, pressing closer, wanting - needing - to eliminate any space between us.

I lose track of time, lost in the sensation of Dakota's lips, the taste of him, the solid warmth of his body against mine. When we finally part, we're both breathless. The sounds of the city come rushing back - a car horn honks in the distance, music thumps from a nearby club, and voices and laughter surround us.

"Wow," I manage, my voice barely above a whisper.

Dakota grins, his forehead resting against mine. "Yeah, wow. We're pretty good at 'wow.'"

For a moment, we just stand there, holding each other. I can feel Dakota's heart racing, matching the frantic beat of my own. Part of me wants to forget the cafe, to suggest we go back to his place or mine. But the responsible part of me, the part that remembers Roman waiting at home and my early shift tomorrow, knows we need to slow down.

"So," I say, reluctantly stepping back but keeping hold of his hand. "You mentioned coffee?"

Dakota's grin widens. "Right, coffee. It's just down here."

As we resume our walk, I can't help but smile. My lips are tingling, my heart is soaring, and for the first time in a long time, I feel truly alive. But a small voice in the back of my mind whispers doubts. What about his upcoming tour? What about my school plans? How can we possibly make this work?

I push these thoughts aside, determined to enjoy the moment. Whatever happens next, I know one thing for certain: this night is changing everything.

The cafe is a cozy hideaway, all exposed brick and soft lighting. We settle into a corner booth, the leather seats creaking slightly as we sit. The aroma of fresh coffee envelops us, and for a moment, I let myself relax into the warmth and comfort of it all.

"So," Dakota says, his fingers lightly drumming on the table. "Tell me more about this nursing program. You seemed excited about it earlier."

I take a sip of my latte, buying time to organize my thoughts. "I am excited. It's something I've wanted to do for a long time. But..." I trail off, the reality of my situation weighing heavily on me.

Dakota reaches across the table, his hand covering mine. "But what?"

And just like that, the dam breaks.

"But everything's changing so fast," I blurt out.

"Shannon's leaving in two weeks. She's been my rock, helping with Roman, and splitting the rent. Without her, I don't know how I'm going to manage."

I take a shaky breath, the words tumbling out faster now. "And the program... it's intense. Full-time classes, clinicals. I'll have to cut back my hours at the diner, which means less money coming in. I've been saving, but with Shannon gone, the rent's going to double."

Dakota listens intently, his brow furrowed in concern. I should stop. I know I'm oversharing, but I can't seem to stem the flow of words.

"And Roman... God, he's only going to be three. He needs me. How can I be a good mother if I'm barely around? But if I don't do this now, when will I? I feel like I'm being pulled in a million different directions and I just... I don't know if I can do it all."

I slump back in my seat, emotionally drained. "I'm sorry," I mumble, staring into my coffee. "I didn't mean to dump all of that on you."

There's a moment of silence, and I'm terrified to look up, sure I'll see regret or pity in Dakota's eyes. But when he speaks, his voice is warm and determined.

"Lauren, look at me."

Reluctantly, I raise my eyes to meet his.

"You have nothing to apologize for," he says firmly. "What you're trying to do... it's fucking incredible. And yeah, it's going to be fucking hard. But from what I've seen, you're one of the strongest fucking people I've ever met." He smirks slightly. "Sorry for all the swearing."

His words touch something deep inside me, and I feel tears prickling at the corners of my eyes.

"I want to help," Dakota continues, a hint of frustration in his voice. "I know I'll be on tour soon after Shannon leaves, so I can't be there physically. But maybe I could... I don't know, help with the rent for a few months? Or set up a fund for childcare?"

"Dakota, no," I interrupt, shaking my head. "I can't accept that. We barely know each other, and it's too much."

He squeezes my hand. "It's not too much. Not for me. I care about you, Lauren. I want to see you succeed. And this... this is something I can do."

I look at him, really look at him, and see nothing but sincerity in his eyes. It's overwhelming, this unexpected offer. Part of me is touched by his generosity, while another part is wary of accepting such significant help from someone I've just started dating. Or anyone, for that matter. I do things on my own. On my own terms. My independence was hard-won. I treasure it. Sometimes I think it's all I have.

"I... I don't know what to say," I finally manage. "It's incredibly generous, but I can't just take your money. It wouldn't feel right."

Dakota nods, looking a bit deflated. "I understand. I just... I wish there was something I could do to make this easier for you."

His genuine desire to help warms my heart, even as I grapple with the complexity of our situation. "You being here, listening to me... that helps more than you know," I say softly.

He smiles, but I can see the concern still lingering in his eyes. "Just know that the offer stands, okay? If you change your mind, or if there's anything else I can do to help, just say the word."

As I nod, with gratitude and uncertainty swirling inside me, I realize that this night has indeed changed everything. For better or worse, Dakota has just become a part of my complicated life. And despite all my fears and doubts, I find myself hoping he'll stay, even as I know he has to leave.

eighteen
here for good

Dakota

The bass line slips away from me again, my fingers fumbling over the strings. I shake my head, trying to clear the fog that seems to have settled over my brain.

"Dakota, man, where are you right now?" Brad's voice cuts through the haze, concern and frustration coloring his words.

I look up to see the rest of Chaos Fuel staring at me. Brad, our lead singer, has his arms crossed, one eyebrow raised in question. Stefan, our guitarist, is frowning, his fingers still poised over his instrument. And Emmett, usually lost in his own world behind the drums, is actually paying attention for once.

"Sorry, guys," I mutter, running a hand through my hair. "I'm just... distracted."

"No shit," Emmett chuckles. "You've been off all week. What gives?"

I hesitate, unsure how much to share. These guys are

my brothers in all but blood, but talking about Lauren feels private.

Stefan, ever the perceptive one, narrows his eyes. "You've been disappearing a lot lately. Is there something going on we should know about?"

I hesitate, unsure how much to share. "I've been spending some time with Lauren," I admit finally.

"Lauren?" Brad repeats, his brow furrowing for a moment before his eyes light up with recognition. "Wait, you mean Lauren from Sunny's? The waitress?"

"Yeah, that's her," I nod, feeling a mix of relief and nervousness at having it out in the open.

"Oh man, I know her," Emmett chimes in. "She always remembers my crazy coffee order. Nice girl."

Stefan leans back, a knowing smirk on his face. "I thought I noticed some sparks flying between you two last time we were there. So, you've been 'spending time' with her, huh?"

I feel heat creep up my neck. "We've been hanging out, yeah. Getting to know each other."

"Must be some pretty intense 'hanging out' to have you this distracted," Emmett quips, twirling a drumstick between his fingers.

Brad's expression turns serious. "Dakota, you know we're leaving for tour soon, right? Opening for Incendiary Ink's farewell tour for three months? Ring any bells?"

The reminder hits me like a slap to the face.

"I know," I say quietly. "Trust me, I know."

Stefan sets his guitar down, his expression serious.

"Look, man, we're happy for you. Really. But we need you focused. This tour... it's huge for us. It could be our big break."

"I know that too," I say, a hint of defensiveness creeping into my voice. "I'm not going to let you guys down."

"We know you won't," Emmett chimes in. "But maybe... maybe you should take a step back from this Lauren situation. At least until after the tour."

His words make sense. They're practical, logical. But the thought of stepping back from Lauren, of not seeing where this could go... it feels wrong on a level I can't quite explain.

"I can't do that," I say, surprising myself with the firmness in my voice.

The guys exchange another look, this one filled with concern and a hint of exasperation.

"Alright," Brad finally says. "But Dakota, you've got to find a way to balance this. We need you here, present, giving it your all. Can you do that?"

I nod, determination settling over me. "Yeah, I can do that. I promise."

"Good," Stefan says. "Now, let's take it from the top. And this time, try to remember you're holding a bass, not daydreaming about your waitress, alright?"

I roll my eyes but can't help the small smile that tugs at my lips. As we launch into the song again, I force myself to focus, to push thoughts of Lauren to the back of my mind.

But even as my fingers find their rhythm on the

strings, I know this is just the beginning. Balancing my growing feelings for Lauren with the demands of the band and the tour ahead... it's going to be one hell of a challenge.

Since I started seeing Lauren, I haven't had the urge to drink or use, and I can only pray that continues once I'm on the road. I'm going to need to find strength I don't know that I have to get through it. I've seen Lauren every single day since we met, and I worry that any amount of distance may be too much for me to handle. I might slip up. I might give in to my demons in a moment of weakness. The temptations on the road are huge and constant. Nearly unavoidable. I'm not sure I have the fortitude to be the man I want so desperately to be.

But as I look around at my bandmates, my brothers, I know I'm not alone. And somehow, someway, I'll find a way to make it all work.

I have to.

The setting sun paints the sky in hues of orange and pink as I pull up to Lauren's house after practice. The air is thick with the scent of jasmine from a nearby bush, mingling with the acrid smell of exhaust from Shannon's idling Honda. Its trunk gapes open, stuffed with boxes and suitcases - a visual reminder of the changes ahead.

My stomach churns with a mix of emotions: sympathy for Lauren's loss, guilt about my own impending departure, and an overwhelming desire to fix everything. But I know I can't. Not really.

I find them in the driveway, Lauren and Shannon engaged in a complicated dance of fitting boxes into the cramped backseat. Roman sits on the porch step, his small shoulders slumped, looking lost in a way no three-year-old should.

"Hey," I call out softly, gravel crunching under my feet as I approach.

Lauren turns, a sad smile flickering across her face. "Dakota, hey. I didn't expect you tonight."

I shrug, shoving my hands in my pockets to stop myself from reaching out to her. "Thought you might need an extra pair of hands. Or, you know, just some moral support."

Shannon emerges from the car, wiping sweat from her brow. "Well, well. If it isn't the rockstar," she says, her usual teasing tone tinged with something harder - worry, maybe, or skepticism.

"Need any help?" I offer, gesturing to the remaining boxes.

"We've got it," Shannon says, her eyes flicking between Lauren and me. "But it's good you're here for Lauren. She'll need support."

The emphasis she puts on "support" isn't lost on me. It's a reminder, a warning perhaps, of the responsibility I'm taking on.

I nod, moving to stand beside Lauren. She leans into me slightly, and I wrap an arm around her shoulders, breathing in the familiar scent of her shampoo.

"You okay?" I murmur low enough that only she can hear.

She nods, but I can feel the tension thrumming through her body. "I will be," she whispers back.

As Shannon loads the last box, I crouch down next to Roman. "Hey, buddy," I say softly. "Tough day, huh?"

He nods, his big brown eyes welling with tears. Without thinking, I open my arms, and he launches himself into them. As I hold him, I'm struck by how right it feels, and how terrifying that rightness is. Soon, I'll be leaving, too. What right do I have to offer comfort I can't sustain?

Shannon's voice breaks through my thoughts. "Well, I guess this is it."

What follows is a flurry of tearful goodbyes. I stand back, an observer to this family's pain, acutely aware of my outsider status even as I long to be a part of it.

As Shannon prepares to leave, she pulls me aside. "Dakota," she says, her voice low and intense. "I know you care about them. But this isn't a game. Lauren and Roman... they can't afford to get hurt. You understand?"

I meet her gaze, feeling the weight of her words. "I do. I promise, I'm not taking this lightly."

She searches my face for a moment, then nods. "Good. Take care of them, okay? They're special."

As Shannon's car disappears into the distance, Lauren's hand finds mine, squeezing tightly. Roman clings to her legs, sniffling quietly. The three of us stand there, a tableau of grief and uncertainty.

"You've got this," I tell Lauren softly, even as doubt gnaws at me. "And I'm here, whatever you need."

She nods, leaning her head against my shoulder. But as the streetlights flicker on around us, I can't shake the feeling that I'm making promises I might not be able to keep. In a short time, I'll be gone, too, chasing my dreams on stage while Lauren faces her new reality alone.

The guilt is overwhelming, but so is the certainty that I can't walk away from this - from her, from them.

nineteen
passacaglia

Lauren

The house feels eerily quiet without Shannon's presence, the silence broken only by the soft hum of the refrigerator and the distant sounds of traffic outside. I lean against Roman's doorframe, watching his little chest rise and fall in the soft glow of his nightlight. His face is still puffy from crying, and dried tear tracks are visible on his cheeks. My heart constricts, knowing this is just the beginning of the changes he'll have to face.

I feel Dakota's presence before I see him, a warmth at my back. His arms slip around my waist, and I lean into him, grateful for his solid strength even as guilt nags at me. Should I be allowing myself this comfort when Roman is hurting?

"He finally asleep?" Dakota murmurs, his breath warm against my ear, sending a shiver down my spine.

I nod, not trusting my voice just yet. Dakota gently tugs me away from the door, and I let him guide me to the living room couch. We sink down together, his arm still around me, my head finding that perfect spot on his shoulder. The leather of the couch creaks softly beneath us, a sound that used to mean Shannon flopping down after a long day.

For a while, we just sit in silence. I listen to the steady thump of Dakota's heartbeat, letting it ground me in this moment. His fingers trace lazy patterns on my arm, each touch igniting a spark under my skin. The scent of his cologne – a mix of sandalwood and something uniquely him – envelops me, comforting and exciting all at once.

"You okay?" he asks softly, breaking the silence.

I take a shaky breath, considering the question. Am I okay? Shannon's gone. I'm facing truly single motherhood with no support, nursing school, and financial struggles. And Dakota... Dakota will be leaving soon, too. "I don't know," I admit finally. "It doesn't feel real yet. Shannon's always been here, you know? And now..."

"Now you're facing a lot of changes," Dakota finishes for me, his voice laced with understanding and something else – regret, maybe?

I nod, turning to look at him. In the dim light of the living room, his eyes are dark, intense. They draw me in, making me forget, just for a moment, about all the complications in our lives. "Dakota, I—"

But before I can finish, his lips are on mine. The kiss is gentle at first, comforting, but it quickly deepens. I respond eagerly, weeks of pent-up emotion and desire pouring out. My hands find their way into his hair, soft strands slipping through my fingers as I pull him closer.

Dakota groans softly, the sound sending heat

coursing through me. His hands slip under the hem of my shirt, warm against my skin, leaving trails of fire in their wake. I arch into his touch, wanting – needing more.

We break apart, both breathing heavily. Dakota rests his forehead against mine, his eyes searching my face. "Lauren," he says, his voice rough with desire but tinged with concern. "Are you sure about this? With everything going on..."

For a moment, reality intrudes. Roman sleeping just down the hall. Dakota leaving for tour soon. The mountain of changes I'm facing. The potential heartbreak looming on the horizon. But looking into Dakota's eyes, seeing the care, the want, the vulnerability there, I make my decision.

I silence him with another kiss, softer this time, pouring all my complicated emotions into it. "I'm sure," I whisper against his lips. "I need this. I need you."

That's all the encouragement Dakota needs. In one fluid motion, he lifts me onto his lap. I straddle him, reveling in the feeling of his strong thighs beneath me, the heat of him pressed against me. As we kiss again, more urgently this time, I'm acutely aware of every point where our bodies connect.

As things heat up between us, a small voice in the back of my mind reminds me of the potential consequences. Are we moving too fast? What if Roman wakes up? What will this mean for us when Dakota leaves?

But for now, I push those thoughts aside. Tonight, I just want to feel. I want to lose myself in Dakota's touch, in the way he makes me feel wanted, cherished, and alive. Tomorrow, I'll face reality. But tonight... tonight is ours.

And as Dakota's hands roam my body, as our kisses grow more heated, I know that whatever comes next, this moment – complicated and messy as it may be – is exactly what I need.

Dakota's hands glide up my sides, taking my shirt with them. I lift my arms, allowing him to pull it off. His eyes roam over me, filled with awe and desire.

"You're beautiful," he whispers, leaning in to trail soft kisses along my collarbone.

I shiver at his touch, my fingers working to unbutton his shirt. As I push it off his shoulders, I take in the sight of his toned chest, and the tattoos that decorate his skin. I trace them with my fingertips, feeling the slight raise of the ink.

Our lips meet again, deeper this time. Dakota's hands find the clasp of my bra, and he looks at me questioningly. I nod, and he gently removes it. His touch is reverent as he explores my newly exposed skin.

I grind against him, feeling his arousal through his jeans. He groans softly, his hands moving to my hips to guide my movements. The friction is delicious, but I want more.

"Bedroom," I breathe against his ear.

Dakota stands, lifting me with him. I wrap my legs around his waist as he carries me down the hall, careful not to make noise as we pass Roman's room.

In my bedroom, he lays me gently on the bed. We take our time undressing each other, pausing to kiss and caress newly revealed skin. When we're finally bare before each other, Dakota hovers over me, his eyes searching mine.

"Are you sure?" he asks again, his voice tender.

In response, I pull him down for a kiss. "I'm sure," I murmur against his lips.

As Dakota enters me, a flood of sensations washes over me. The stretch, the fullness, the warmth of his skin against mine - it's overwhelming in the best way. But it's more than just physical. There's an emotional intensity that takes my breath away.

For a moment, we're still, foreheads pressed together, sharing the same breath. I open my eyes to find Dakota watching me, his gaze so tender it makes my heart ache. In his eyes, I see desire, yes, but also understanding, care, and something deeper that I'm not ready to name.

"Lauren," he whispers, his voice rough with emotion. His hand cups my cheek, thumb gently stroking my skin. "You feel like coming home."

The words hit me hard, bringing tears to my eyes. Home. It's been so long since I've felt that sense of belonging, of rightness. And now, with Shannon gone and everything changing, I need this more than ever.

We begin to move together, finding a gentle rhythm. Dakota's touches are reverent, as if he's committing every inch of me to memory. His calloused fingertips, a testament to years of playing bass, trail fire across my skin. I run my hands along his back, feeling the play of muscles, tracing the lines of the tattoo I know spans his shoulders

- a phoenix rising from the ashes, a symbol of his own rebirth.

Our pace gradually increases, but it never loses that sense of tenderness. The room fills with the sound of our ragged breathing, soft moans, and the whisper of skin against skin. The scent of Dakota's cologne mingles with the heat of our lovemaking, creating an intoxicating mix.

As we near the edge, Dakota's hand finds mine, our fingers intertwining. "Look at me," he murmurs, and I do, locking eyes with him as pleasure builds. In that moment of connection, I feel seen, truly seen, in a way I haven't in years.

We fall over the edge together, clinging to each other as waves of ecstasy wash over us. I cry out softly, mindful of Roman sleeping down the hall, as Dakota buries his face in my neck, his body shuddering against mine.

Afterward, we lie tangled together, my head on his chest, listening to his heartbeat slowly return to normal. Dakota presses a kiss to my forehead, his arms tightening around me protectively.

In this moment, despite all the uncertainty ahead, I feel safe, cherished, and completely at peace. But as the afterglow fades, reality begins to creep back in. Dakota will be leaving soon. This bubble we've created can't last forever.

As if sensing my thoughts, Dakota tilts my chin up, meeting my eyes. "Hey," he says softly. "Where'd you go just now?"

I bite my lip, debating whether to voice my fears. But looking into his eyes, which are so full of warmth and understanding, I find the courage to be honest. "I was just thinking... what happens now? When you leave for tour?"

Dakota's arms tighten around me, and I feel him take a deep breath. "I don't know," he admits. "But I do know this - what we have, it's special. I'm not fucking walking away from it. We'll figure it out, okay?"

I nod, wanting desperately to believe him. For now, I push the worries aside and snuggle closer, letting the steady beat of Dakota's heart lull me. Tomorrow, we'll face reality. But tonight... tonight is ours.

twenty
kiss from a rose

Dakota

The soft light of dawn filters through Lauren's curtains. I trace my fingers lightly along her arm, committing every detail to memory. Her hair is tousled from sleep, her lips slightly parted. The sight of her makes my chest ache in a way I haven't felt in years.

I should leave. Roman will be up soon, and although he knows me, Lauren and I agreed it's best not to complicate things further right now. But I can't seem to make myself move.

Lauren stirs, her eyes fluttering open. A slow smile spreads across her face as she focuses on me. "Morning," she murmurs, voice husky with sleep.

"Morning," I whisper back, leaning in to brush a soft kiss against her lips.

She glances at the clock and sighs. "You should probably go soon."

"Yeah," I agree, but I make no move to get up. Instead, I pull her closer, burying my face in her hair.

Lauren chuckles softly. "Dakota..."

"I know, I know," I groan, finally forcing myself to sit up. I reach for my jeans on the floor, but as I do, a melody starts to form in my head. Fragments of lyrics follow, raw and unfiltered.

I grab my phone from the nightstand, opening the voice memo app. "Hold on," I mutter to Lauren, hitting record.

I hum the melody softly, then whisper-sing:

"Ghosts of the past, always at our heels
Scars still raw, time hasn't healed
But in this moment, between night
    and day
We found a shelter, where shadows fade
    away"

I pause the recording, the weight of the words hanging in the air. It's not perfect, but it's honest. It captures the complexity of what's growing between us, acknowledging our pasts while celebrating this fragile new beginning.

Lauren props herself up on an elbow, watching me with a mix of curiosity and something deeper. "New song?"

I nod, suddenly feeling exposed. "Just trying to capture this. Us. It's not finished, obviously."

She reaches out, running her fingers through my hair. "It's beautiful," she says softly. "And a little haunting."

I lean into her touch, closing my eyes. "That's us, isn't it? Beautiful and a little haunting."

A creak in the hallway makes us both freeze. We hold our breath, listening. After a moment, we hear the soft patter of little feet heading towards the bathroom.

"Time's up," I mutter, scrambling out of bed. I pull on my jeans and search for my shirt, finding it tangled in the sheets.

Lauren helps me dress, her movements quick but her touch lingering. As I shrug on my jacket, she pulls me in for one last, fierce kiss.

"Call me later?" she asks, a hint of vulnerability in her voice.

I cup her face in my hands, meeting her eyes. "Count on it. This isn't goodbye. It's just... see you later."

She nods, a small smile tugging at her lips. I give her one last quick kiss before slipping out of the bedroom.

I make it to the front door just as I hear Roman's voice calling out, "Mommy?"

As I step outside, closing the door quietly behind me, I feel a pang in my chest. Part of me wants to stay, to ruffle Roman's hair and see his gap-toothed grin. But I know Lauren's right – we need to take this slow, for Roman's sake as much as our own.

I head to my car, already missing the warmth of Lauren's bed, of Lauren herself. But as I slide behind the wheel, I find myself humming the new melody. I may be leaving, but I'm taking something with me – the start of a new song, and the promise of something real with Lauren.

I pull out my phone again, adding one last line before I drive away:

*"In this limbo between healing and pain
We dare to hope, to feel alive again"*

The words still aren't perfect, but they're true. And for now, that's enough.

The streets of LA are surprisingly quiet as I drive to our practice space. My fingers tap out the rhythm of the new song on the steering wheel, my mind still back in Lauren's house.

I pull into the parking lot of the nondescript warehouse we rent. Brad's car is already there. Perfect. I grab my bass and the notebook where I scribbled down the lyrics, then head inside.

The familiar smell of stale beer and amp dust greets me as I push open the door. Brad's sitting on a beat-up couch, acoustic guitar in hand, looking up as I enter.

"Morning, sunshine," he grins. "You look like you've had an interesting night."

I glance down at myself briefly, not seeing anything too crazy, a little wrinkled maybe. "Why's that?"

"You haven't changed clothes since yesterday."

I roll my eyes but can't hide my smile. "Whatever. Listen, I've got something I want to run by you."

Brad raises an eyebrow, setting his guitar aside. "Oh? Let's hear it."

I pull out my phone, playing the voice memo I recorded at Lauren's. As the rough melody and lyrics fill the room, I watch Brad's face. His expression shifts from curiosity to concentration, fingers tapping out the rhythm on his knee.

When it ends, he nods slowly, scratching at his dark blonde beard. "There's definitely something there. It's different from our usual stuff, but... I like it. It's raw. Real."

"Yeah," I agree, sitting down next to him. "I think it could be something special."

Brad gives me a knowing look. "This about that waitress? Lauren, right?"

I nod, suddenly finding the frayed edge of my jeans very interesting. "Yeah. We, uh... things are getting serious."

"I can tell," Brad says softly. Then he sighs. "Look, Dakota... you know I'm happy for you, right? But the tour..."

"I know," I cut him off. "Believe me, I know. But this... it feels different, Brad. She's different."

Brad's quiet for a moment, strumming a few chords absently. "You haven't really gotten serious with anyone since Chloe, have you?"

I shake my head, feeling the familiar ache at the mention of my late wife. "No. Didn't feel right. Until now."

"Being on the road, it's tough on relationships," Brad

says gently. "Even established ones. And you're just starting out with Lauren."

I run a hand through my hair, frustration bubbling up. "So what, I shouldn't even fucking try? Just stick to groupies and one-night stands forever?"

"That's not what I'm saying," Brad says calmly. "I'm saying you need to be prepared. Set expectations. Communicate. And most importantly, don't let it affect the band."

I nod slowly, knowing he's right. "Any tips from the Brad Chambers guide to long-distance relationships?"

He chuckles. "Schedule regular calls, no matter how busy things get. Be honest about the temptations on the road, but reassure her, too. And maybe... write her songs. Not just sad, missing-you songs, but ones that make her feel like she's there with you."

I smile, feeling some of the tension ease from my shoulders. "Thanks, man. I appreciate it."

Brad claps me on the shoulder. "Anytime. Now, let's see if we can turn this love-struck rambling of yours into an actual song, yeah?"

The rehearsal space buzzes with pre-tour energy. Emmett's tapping out a restless beat on his practice pad, Stefan's fiddling with his guitar pedals, and Brad's warming up his voice in the corner. But I'm only half-listening as Ian, our manager, goes over the tour itinerary.

"So, we'll kick off in San Diego, then head up the

coast," Ian's saying, his British accent thick as his finger traces the route on a map. "We've got two nights in San Francisco, then it's on to Portland..."

My pen moves across my notebook, but it's not tour dates I'm jotting down. It's more lyrics, fragments of another melody that's been haunting me for days.

Her smile like a sunrise, breaking through
    the dark
A beacon of hope, igniting a spark
In a world of chaos, I'm safe in her arms
In a sea of doubt, she's my calm

"Dakota? You with us, man?"

I snap back to attention, realizing everyone's looking at me. "Yeah, sorry. Just, uh, working on some lyrics."

Brad raises an eyebrow. "Another new song?"

I nod, feeling a flush creep up my neck. "Maybe. It's still pretty fucking rough."

Ian clears his throat, looking mildly annoyed. "As I was saying, we've got a string of Midwest dates after Chicago. It's going to be a grueling schedule, so I need everyone focused."

I nod, trying to concentrate. But my mind keeps drifting back to Lauren. To her laugh, her resilience, the way her eyes light up when she talks about her dreams.

She's a symphony in a world of noise
A melody that brings me joy
With every note, every line

She makes this broken heart of mine
Feel alive, feel alive

"Alright, let's run through the setlist," Brad says, breaking me out of my reverie. "Dakota, you good to start with *'Midnight Mirage'*?"

I nod, setting aside my notebook and picking up my bass. As we launch into the song, I try to focus on the music, on the rhythm, and the interplay with my bandmates. But even as my fingers find the familiar notes, part of me is still with Lauren.

Three months. Three months on the road, away from her, from the connection we've been building. It feels like a fucking eternity.

As we finish the song, Stefan gives me a knowing look. "So, this new song... it wouldn't happen to be about a certain waitress, would it?"

I feel my cheeks heat up. "Maybe."

Emmett grins. "Man, you've got it bad."

"Alright, alright," Brad interjects, but he's smiling too. "Let's focus, guys. We've got a tour to prepare for."

As we dive back into rehearsal, I can't help but sneak glances at my notebook. The lyrics might be rough, the melody still forming, but the feeling behind them... that's real.

That's powerful.

And for the first time in years, I'm excited to see where these songs - and this relationship - might lead.

I finally have a muse.

twenty-one
goddess

Lauren

T he campus bustles with activity as I navigate the parking lot, Roman's hand firmly in mine. The admissions building looms ahead, a mix of excitement and anxiety churning in my stomach.

"Mommy, are we seeing the fish tanks again?" Roman asks, tugging at my hand.

I smile, remembering his fascination with the marine biology department's aquariums during our last visit. "Not today, sweetie. We're going to check out that special place I told you about, where you might spend time while Mommy's in class."

Inside the admissions office, I spot Deborah, the kind woman who helped me with my application paperwork. She waves us over with a smile.

"Lauren, good to see you again. And this must be Roman," she says, crouching down to his level. "I hear you're quite the fish expert."

Roman nods shyly, a small smile tugging at his lips.

As Deborah finalizes my enrollment documents, my phone buzzes. It's a text from Shannon.

> SHANNON: Just crossed into Oregon. How are my two favorite people holding up?

I type back quickly.

> ME: Hanging in there. At the college checking out the daycare. Drive safe. Call when you can.

"And you're all set for the student daycare tour?" Deborah asks, bringing my attention back.

I nod eagerly. "Yes, we're really looking forward to it."

She makes a quick call, then leads us across the familiar campus to a cheery building with a playground out front. Inside, the walls are covered in children's artwork, and the sound of laughter fills the air.

Ms. Patel, the daycare director, greets us warmly. As she shows us around, Roman's initial hesitation fades. By the time we reach the preschool room, he's eagerly exploring the toy area.

"Remember, Roman," I say gently, "this isn't for today. But you might spend time here when Mommy starts her classes."

He nods, already engrossed in a colorful puzzle.

"We have a few spots still available for the fall semester, so you're in luck," Ms. Patel explains. "The hours align with classes, and we offer extended care for study groups or lab work."

Relief washes over me. This could work. This could actually work.

As we leave campus, my phone rings. It's Shannon.

"Hey, road warrior," I answer, putting it on speaker as I buckle Roman into his car seat. "How's the drive?"

"Long," Shannon sighs. "But the scenery's beautiful. How did the daycare tour go?"

"Good! Roman, want to tell Aunt Shannon about the cool toys you saw?"

As Roman chatters excitedly about the daycare, I feel a lump form in my throat. It's only been a day, but Shannon's absence is palpable.

"Lauren?" Shannon's voice brings me back. "You okay?"

I take a deep breath. "Yeah, just... it's a lot. But we're managing."

"I know you are," Shannon's voice is warm. "You're the strongest person I know, cuz. You've got this."

We talk for a few more minutes before saying good-bye, Shannon promising to call when she reaches her new apartment in Seattle.

As I hang up, I notice a text message.

DAKOTA: Hope your day's going well.
Can I call you later?

A smile tugs at my lips despite the stress.

ME: Looking forward to it!

The alarm blares at 2 PM, pulling me from a fitful nap. I groan, fumbling to silence it. The events of the morning - the campus visit, the daycare tour, Shannon's call - swirl in my mind, mixing with memories of last night with Dakota.

I force myself out of bed. No time to dwell on any of that now. I need to get Roman ready for his first day at Little Sprouts Daycare.

"Roman, sweetie," I call, knocking on his door. "Time to wake up from your nap."

He emerges, rubbing his eyes sleepily. "Is it time for the new daycare, Mommy?"

I nod, kneeling down to his level. "That's right, buddy. Remember, this is a different one from the one we saw this morning. But I bet it'll be just as fun."

Roman's lower lip trembles slightly. "Will you stay with me?"

My heart clenches. "I can't stay, sweetie. I have to go to work. But I promise I'll pick you up as soon as I'm done."

The next hour is a whirlwind of getting dressed, eating a quick snack, and packing bags. By the time we're in the car, heading to Little Sprouts Daycare, I'm already feeling the pressure of our new schedule.

We pull up to the cheerful building with its colorful playground. As I help Roman out of his car seat, a knot forms in my stomach. Is this too much change too fast?

Inside, we're greeted by a smiling woman with kind

eyes. "You must be Roman! I'm Miss Jess. We're so excited to have you join us for our afternoon program."

Roman clings to my leg, suddenly shy. I crouch down beside him. "Remember how brave you were this morning at the college daycare? You can be brave here, too. And look at all the cool toys they have!"

After a few more minutes of gentle coaxing, Roman agrees to join Miss Jess in feeding the class fish. As they walk away, he glances back once, waving. I wave back, maintaining my smile until they turn the corner.

Back in the car, I let out a shaky breath. The events of the past 24 hours crash over me - Shannon leaving, the night with Dakota, the morning at the college, and now this new step for Roman. It's all happening so fast.

As I drive to Sunny's for my dinner shift, my mind races. There's so much to juggle - work, the upcoming school, Roman's schedules, finances. And then there's Dakota, this unexpected bright spot in the chaos of my life. But he'll be leaving for tour soon.

I park outside Sunny's, taking a moment to collect myself. This is only the first day of massive change. An introduction of what's yet to come, and already I'm exhausted. I haven't even started classes yet. I don't know if I can do this.

The diner is already bustling when I clock in at 4 PM. I tie on my apron and jump right in, taking over from the afternoon shift.

The next few hours are a whirlwind of orders, spills, and the controlled chaos of the dinner rush. I weave between tables, refilling drinks, delivering steaming plates, and managing the Friday night crowd.

Around 7 PM, during a brief lull, I check my phone. No missed calls from the daycare - a good sign. There's another text from Dakota.

> DAKOTA: Writing session with Brad went great. Wish you could hear it.

I smile, warmth spreading through my chest. Then I guiltily shove the phone back in my pocket as the bell above the door chimes, signaling new customers.

The rest of the shift flies by in a blur of coffee refills, burger orders, and friendly chatter with regulars. By the time 9 PM rolls around, my feet are aching, and I'm running on fumes.

I rush to my car, heart pounding as I drive to Little Sprouts. I'm the last parent to arrive, and guilt gnaws at me as I see Roman sitting with Miss Jess, looking small and tired.

"Mommy!" he cries, running to me. I scoop him up, peppering his face with kisses.

"I'm so sorry I'm late, buddy. Did you have a good time?"

He nods sleepily against my shoulder. Miss Jess gives me a kind smile. "He did great for his first day. We'll see you both on Monday?"

I nod, grateful for her understanding. As we drive home, Roman already dozing in his car seat, my phone buzzes. It's Dakota. "You free to talk?"

I smile despite my exhaustion. "Give me 20 minutes to get Roman to bed?"

"Take your time," he replies. "I'll be here."

Tucking Roman in, I reflect on the day. It was hard, no doubt. But we did it. Roman survived his first day at the new daycare. I managed work. And now, I have Dakota's call to look forward to.

One day at a time, I remind myself. We can do this.

twenty-two
coincidences

Dakota

I stare at my phone, thumb hovering over Lauren's name. The urge to hear her voice again is almost overwhelming, but suddenly, a phone call doesn't feel like enough. Before I can overthink it, I'm grabbing my keys and heading out the door. I can get there in twenty minutes. No problem.

The late-night traffic in LA is mercifully light. As I drive, my mind wanders back to this morning - sneaking out of Lauren's house, the new songs forming in my head, the productive writing session with Brad. It's been a whirlwind of a day, but Lauren's been at the center of my thoughts throughout.

I stop at an all-night grocery store, picking up a modest bouquet of daisies and carnations. Nothing too over-the-top, I think, just something to brighten her night after a long day.

As I pull up to her house, doubt creeps in. What if

she's already asleep? What if Roman's still awake and I'm intruding? What if this is too much, too soon?

I shake off the doubts and make my way to her door. Taking a deep breath, I knock softly.

There's a moment of silence, then the sound of footsteps. The door opens, and Lauren stands there, eyes wide with surprise. She's in pajama pants and an old t-shirt, her hair pulled back in a messy bun. There are dark circles under her eyes, and she looks utterly exhausted. But to me, she's never looked more beautiful.

"Dakota?" she says, her voice a mix of confusion and pleasure. "What are you doing here?"

I hold out the flowers, suddenly feeling a bit sheepish. "I, uh, I wanted to surprise you. See how your day went in person."

Lauren's eyes soften as she takes in the flowers, but I can see the self-consciousness creep into her expression. She runs a hand over her hair, tugging at her shirt. "I'm a mess," she says with a nervous laugh. "I wasn't expecting... I mean, I just put Roman to bed, and I haven't even showered yet, and-"

I step forward, gently cupping her face with my free hand. "Hey," I say softly, cutting off her rambling. "You look perfect to me. I'm the one who showed up unannounced, remember?"

She leans into my touch, some of the tension leaving her shoulders. "You're sure? I mean, this isn't exactly how I pictured our next meeting going."

I chuckle, leaning in to press a soft kiss to her forehead. "Lauren, I've seen you at 6 AM with bedhead and morning breath. Trust me, this? This is perfect."

A smile finally breaks through her worry. "Well, in that case," she says, stepping back and opening the door wider, "come on in. But be quiet - I just got Roman to sleep, and if he wakes up now, I might cry."

As I step inside, I can feel the weariness radiating off her. But there's also a warmth, a sense of home that I've missed all day. I hand her the flowers, watching as she brings them to her nose, inhaling deeply.

"Thank you," she says softly. "They're beautiful."

"Not as beautiful as you," I reply, then cringe internally at how cheesy it sounds. But Lauren's smile widens, a blush coloring her cheeks.

"Smooth talker," she teases, then yawns widely. "Sorry, it's been a long day."

I nod, suddenly unsure. "I can go if you're too tired. I just... I wanted to see you."

Lauren reaches out, taking my hand and squeezing it gently. "Stay," she says simply. "I'm tired, but I want to see you too."

After putting the flowers in some water, she leads me to the couch, and I can see the mix of exhaustion and happiness in her eyes. I know, without a doubt, that this surprise visit was the right call.

We settle onto the couch, Lauren curling into my side as I drape my arm around her shoulders. She grabs the remote, flipping through Netflix options.

"Something light?" she suggests, stifling another

yawn. "I don't think my brain can handle anything too complex right now."

I chuckle, giving her shoulder a gentle squeeze. "Sounds perfect. How about something classic?"

As we scroll through options, a comfortable silence falls between us. Lauren's warmth against me is soothing, and I find myself relaxing for the first time all day.

We settle on an old episode of "Law & Order." It's familiar enough that we don't need to focus too hard, but engaging enough to keep us awake. As the episode progresses, it becomes clear that it's about a pair of seemingly unrelated deaths that turn out to be connected.

The episode unfolds, and Lauren shifts against me, her body tensing slightly.

"You okay?" I ask softly.

She nods, then hesitates. "Yeah, just... this episode. It made me think of something."

I raise an eyebrow, encouraging her to continue.

Lauren takes a deep breath. "It's probably nothing, but... You know how we both mentioned losing Miles and Chloe about three years ago?"

I nod, recalling our previous conversations. "Yeah..."

"Right," she confirms. "I was pregnant with Roman at the time. Miles and I... we were fighting a lot."

A thought strikes me. "You know, I don't think we ever actually compared dates. I know it was May 6th for Chloe, but..."

Lauren's eyes widen slightly. "May 6th? That's the same day Miles died."

My heart rate picks up, but I try to keep my voice calm. "Really? That's a coincidence."

Lauren nods slowly. "Yeah, it is. I never got many details about what happened. Since we weren't married, I wasn't really considered family. And in LA..."

"People OD all the time," I finish for her, a bitter taste in my mouth. "Not a lot of investigating goes into it."

"Exactly," Lauren says softly.

"I always assumed Chloe was at our dealer's house when it happened. I was on tour, and..."

"And I was staying with Shannon," Lauren finishes. "I never knew exactly where Miles was that night. I just got the call from a friend of his that said he died at St. Francis Hospital."

"St. Francis?" I ask, the coincidences becoming too real. "That's where—" I don't even say it. Of course, that was where Chloe died, too. Or, at least, where she was pronounced dead.

We fall silent, the weight of these realizations hanging between us. The TV drones on in the background, forgotten. My mind is racing, curiosity burning inside me, but I force myself to remain outwardly calm.

"It's probably just a coincidence," I say, trying to sound convincing. "I mean, what are the fucking odds, right?"

Lauren nods, but she looks uncertain. "Yeah, probably. With everything going on with the pregnancy and the grief, I guess I never questioned it too deeply."

We sit in silence for a moment, both lost in our

thoughts. I'm itching to ask more questions, to dig deeper, but I don't want to upset Lauren or disrupt the peace we've found.

"Do you think it matters?" Lauren asks softly, her tone more uncertain than anxious.

I shrug, pulling her closer, even as my mind whirs with possibilities. "I don't know. Maybe it's just a sad coincidence. But if you ever want to talk more about it, about Miles, I'm here."

She smiles up at me, gratitude in her eyes. "Thanks. Same goes for you, about Chloe. When you're ready."

I press a kiss to her forehead, pushing down my burning curiosity. "For now, let's just focus on us, on the present. The past... it'll still be there if we ever decide to look into it more."

Lauren nods, snuggling closer. "I like that plan. Us, in the present."

As we turn our attention back to the TV, I feel a tumult of emotions. There are so many questions about that night three years ago, more now than ever before. But right now, with Lauren in my arms, those questions can wait. We've both been through enough. For now, this moment, this connection we're building, is what matters most.

But in the back of my mind, a spark has been lit. May 6th. Someday, I'll need to know more.

twenty-three
stick around

Lauren

The clock on my dashboard hits 9:15 PM as I pull into Little Sprouts Daycare. My feet ache from the long dinner shift at Sunny's, but the sight of Roman's sleepy face as Miss Jess leads him out washes away some of the exhaustion.

"Mommy," he mumbles, rubbing his eyes as he toddles towards me.

"Hey, baby," I murmur, scooping him up. His weight is familiar and comforting against my hip.

"Good night, Lauren," Miss Jess calls with a wave. "See you tomorrow."

I nod gratefully, inhaling the familiar scent of crayons and disinfectant that always clings to Roman after a day at Little Sprouts. Once again, I'm thankful for this daycare that understands the needs of shift workers like me.

As I buckle Roman into his car seat, my mind races with everything I need to do. Dakota's coming over after his final band practice. Tomorrow, he leaves for three months on tour. Meanwhile, I'm juggling work, Roman, and the looming shadow of nursing school starting soon.

The drive home is quiet, and Roman is already dozing off again. By the time we get home, it's nearly 10. I carry him inside, my arms protesting after a long day of carrying trays.

"Okay, little man," I whisper, gently changing him into pajamas. "Time for bed."

He stirs slightly as I tuck him in. "Dakota?" he mumbles.

My heart clenches, and I hesitate. Part of me wants to promise Roman he'll see Dakota tomorrow, but another part - the protective mother in me - holds back. Dakota's leaving for months. What if things change? What if Roman gets too attached?

"We'll see, sweetie," I finally say, my voice soft. "Let's just focus on getting some sleep now, okay?"

Roman nods, already drifting off again. I press a kiss to his forehead and slip out of the room, guilt and uncertainty settling in my stomach like a stone.

Alone in the living room, I finally have a moment to breathe. I glance at my phone to see a text from Dakota.

> DAKOTA: Just finished practice.
> Heading your way. See you soon. x

My heart flutters, a mix of excitement and anxiety. I look around, suddenly aware of the toys scattered across the floor and the pile of unfolded laundry on the couch. With a sigh, I start tidying up, my mind racing.

How are we going to make this work with him on the road? How will I manage school and Roman without Shannon around? And can I really afford the new daycare I'll need once classes start? Can I afford any of this?

As I fold a tiny t-shirt, my eyes catch the calendar on the kitchen wall. May's page stares back at me, that circled date - the 6th - seeming to pulse with unspoken questions. The day Miles died. The day Dakota's wife died. The day that changed both our lives forever and now, somehow, has brought us together.

A shiver runs through me as I consider the strange twists of fate that led us here. Part of me wants to ask Dakota about it, to unravel this mystery that connects us. But another part is terrified of what we might uncover. With everything else going on - the tour, school, Roman - do we really need to dig up the past?

I shake my head, pushing those thoughts aside. There are more pressing matters to deal with right now. Dakota will be here any minute, and we have a future to figure out.

The sound of a car pulling up outside makes me pause. My heart starts racing, and I feel a flush creep up my neck. I take a deep breath, trying to calm my nerves, and give the living room one last quick scan. It's not perfect, but it'll have to do. I smooth down my hair and walk to the door, my hand hesitating for just a moment on the handle before I pull it open.

Dakota stands there with a weary smile on his face. "Hey, beautiful," he says softly.

"Hey yourself," I reply, stepping back to let him in. "Roman's asleep, so we've got some time to talk."

Dakota nods, his expression turning serious as he follows me to the living room. "Yeah," he agrees. "We've got a lot to figure out."

As we settle onto the couch, I take a deep breath. "So," I begin, my voice shakier than I'd like, "how do we do this? With you on tour and me starting school and everything else..."

Dakota reaches for my hand, his touch grounding me. "That's what we need to figure out," he says. "Together."

Dakota's hand is warm in mine, his thumb tracing gentle circles on my palm. It's soothing, but it can't completely calm the storm of worries in my mind.

"I've been thinking about this a lot," Dakota starts, his voice low. "Three months is a long time, but we can make it work. We've got phones, video calls..."

"It's not just the distance," I interrupt, the words tumbling out before I can stop them. "It's everything. Dakota, I'm starting nursing school. I'll have a new daycare schedule for Roman, and new expenses. Shannon's gone, so I don't have her to lean on anymore. And you'll be out there, living this rockstar life while I'm here just... struggling to keep it all together."

I pause, catching my breath. Dakota's watching me intently, his brow furrowed with concern.

"I'm sorry," I whisper. "I didn't mean to dump all that on you. My anxiety about everything is just getting to me."

He shakes his head, squeezing my hand. "No, don't apologize. This is exactly what we need to talk about. Lauren, I know it's going to be hard. But I'm committed to making this work. To being there for you and Roman, even when I'm not physically here."

"How?" I ask, hating how small my voice sounds.

Dakota takes a deep breath. "Well, for starters, we'll video call every day, even if it's just for a few minutes. I want to hear about your classes, about Roman's day. And I promise, the moment this tour is over, I'm all yours. I'll help with Roman, I'll quiz you for your nursing exams, whatever you need."

His words paint a picture of a future I desperately want to believe in. But there's still a nagging doubt.

"And what about when you're on the road?" I ask, my voice barely above a whisper. My real fears finally coming to the surface. "The parties, the temptations... Dakota, your sobriety. You've worked so hard, and I know you relapsed right before we met. I'm scared for you."

His expression turns serious, a flicker of pain crossing his features. "I know," he says softly. "I'm scared too. But Lauren, I'm committed to staying sober. No after-parties for me. I'm focusing on the music, on why we're really out there."

He meets my gaze steadily. "I can't promise it'll be easy, but I can promise you that I'm doing everything I can to stay on track. I will try my fucking hardest. This... what we're building, it means everything to me. I won't jeopardize that."

I search his face, looking for any sign of hesitation. All I see is sincerity and determination, but I can't help worrying.

"Okay," I say softly. "Just please be careful. And call me anytime if you're struggling. Even if it's the middle of the night."

Dakota nods, squeezing my hand. "I will, I promise." He pauses, then adds hesitantly, "Lauren, I know you said no before, but I want to offer again. Let me help out financially while I'm gone. With school starting and the new daycare, I know things will be tight."

I feel a surge of pride and stubbornness. "Dakota, I appreciate that, I really do. But I need to do this on my own. I've managed this far, and I'll figure it out. It's important to me."

He looks like he wants to argue, but instead, he nods. "I understand. But the offer stands if you change your mind, okay?"

"Okay," I agree, knowing I won't. "Thank you."

"There's one more thing," I say, taking a deep breath. "Promise me you'll be careful with Roman's heart. He's already asking about you, and I just... I can't bear the thought of him getting hurt if this doesn't work out."

Dakota's expression softens. "I promise," he says solemnly. "I care about him too, you know. Both of you. We'll take it slow, and I'll follow your lead when it comes to Roman."

I nod, feeling some of the tension leave my body. There are still a million things to figure out, but for now, this feels like a start.

"So," Dakota says, a small smile playing on his lips as he squeezes my hand. "We're doing this?"

Despite everything, I find myself smiling back. "Yeah," I reply. "We're doing this."

As soon as the words leave my mouth, I feel a mix of emotions wash over me. There's relief, yes, and a surge of warmth as Dakota pulls me into a tight hug. But there's also a flutter of anxiety in my chest, a voice in the back of my mind wondering if I'm making the right choice. For Roman. For myself.

But as I breathe in Dakota's familiar scent, feeling the solid warmth of his body against mine, I push those doubts aside. We might not have all the answers right now, but we're in this together. And for the first time in a long time, I don't feel quite so alone.

I pull back slightly, meeting Dakota's gaze. "It won't be easy," I say softly.

He nods, his eyes serious but warm. "Nothing worth having ever is. But we've got this, Lauren. You and me."

And in that moment, I let myself believe him.

Lord, help me. I believe him.

twenty-four
nfwmb

Dakota

T he pale light of dawn is just beginning to creep through the curtains when I stir awake. For a moment, I'm disoriented, but then I feel Lauren's warm body pressed against mine, and everything clicks into place. I'm in her bed. It's tour day.

I glance at the alarm clock on the nightstand. 5:17 AM. We've got maybe an hour before Roman wakes up, before the day truly begins, and I have to leave.

Lauren shifts in her sleep, her dark hair splayed across the pillow like spun silk in the dim light. I trace the curve of her shoulder with my fingertips, marveling at how quickly she's become essential to me. How am I supposed to leave her for three months?

As if sensing my thoughts, her eyes flutter open. "Dakota?" she murmurs, voice thick with sleep.

"I'm here," I whisper, pulling her closer. "We've still got a little time."

She nods, understanding passing between us without

words. Her hand finds my face, thumb stroking my cheek as she leans in to kiss me. It's soft at first, tentative, but quickly deepens into something more urgent.

We both know what this is - a goodbye, a promise, a moment to hold onto during the long weeks ahead. As I lose myself in Lauren's touch, I try to memorize every detail, every sensation. I want to carry this moment with me on the road, a talisman against loneliness and temptation.

Lauren's lips grow hungrier and more insistent. Her body arches against me, skin warm and soft under my roaming hands. I trace the familiar curves of her hips, her breasts, savoring each touch as if it's our last.

The scent of her fills my nostrils - a mix of her lavender shampoo and something uniquely Lauren. I breathe her in deeply, wanting to memorize this smell, to carry it with me on the long nights ahead.

"Dakota," she breathes, her voice husky with desire. "I need you."

The sound of my name on her lips sends a shiver down my spine. I don't need to be told twice. In one fluid motion, I roll her onto her back, settling between her thighs. She wraps her legs around my waist, pulling me closer. I can feel how ready she is, how much she wants this – wants me.

When I finally push into her, we both gasp. The sensation is overwhelming, perfect. I start to move, slowly at first, then build to a steady rhythm. Lauren meets me thrust for thrust, her nails digging into my back.

"God, Lauren," I groan, burying my face in the crook of her neck. The taste of her skin is intoxicating as I trail kisses along her collarbone.

She responds by clenching around me, eliciting another moan. We move together, finding that perfect sync we've discovered in the short time we've been together. The room fills with the sound of our ragged breathing, punctuated by soft gasps and groans.

A fleeting thought of the tour flashes through my mind, but Lauren's touch quickly pulls me back to the present. Right now, there's only this - her skin against mine, her breath hot on my neck, the powerful rhythm of our bodies moving as one.

I can feel Lauren getting close, her breathing becoming more erratic, her movements more frantic. I slip a hand between us, finding that sensitive spot that drives her wild.

"Come for me, baby," I whisper in her ear. "I've got you."

She does, spectacularly, biting down on my shoulder to muffle her cries. The feel of her pulsing around me sends me over the edge, and I follow her into blissful oblivion.

As we come down from our shared high, I hold Lauren close, our bodies still entwined. The room is quiet except for our gradually slowing breaths. I press a gentle kiss to her forehead, tasting the slight saltiness of sweat on her skin.

"I love you," I murmur, the words slipping out before

I can stop them. It's the first time I've said it, and for a moment, I tense, wondering if it's too soon.

Lauren pulls back slightly, her dark eyes searching mine. A slow smile spreads across her face. "I love you too," she whispers back, and the relief and joy that flood through me are almost overwhelming.

We lie there for a few more precious minutes, trading soft kisses and gentle caresses, until the harsh beeping of the alarm clock shatters our bubble.

Reality crashes back in.

Tour day.

With a sigh, I disentangle myself from Lauren and sit up. "I should get ready," I say, my voice rough.

Lauren nods, sitting up as well. She wraps the sheet around herself, suddenly looking vulnerable. "Yeah, I need to get Roman up soon anyway."

As I start to dress, a familiar pre-tour energy begins to hum through me. Part of me is itching to get on the road, to feel the rush of performing night after night. But for the first time, that excitement is tempered by a strong pull to stay right here, with Lauren and Roman.

I don't want to fucking go.

We move around each other in a kind of dance as we get dressed, stealing glances and touches. The air feels heavy with unspoken words and emotions.

Finally, I'm packed and standing by the front door. Lauren stands before me, Roman on her hip, still sleepy-eyed and clutching his stuffed dinosaur.

"So," I say, my throat tight. "This is it."

Lauren nods, her eyes shining with unshed tears. "Yeah. This is it."

I lean in and kiss her, trying to pour everything I'm feeling into that one gesture. When we part, I ruffle Roman's hair gently. "Be good for your mom, little man. I'll see you soon."

As I walk to my car, I hear the door close behind me. It takes everything in me not to turn back. I slide behind the wheel, taking a deep breath to steady myself.

Three months. I can do this. We can do this.

With one last look at Lauren's house, I start the engine and pull away. The silence in the car is deafening, a stark contrast to the warmth I've just left behind. I reach for the radio, needing something to fill the void.

As the opening chords of our new single fill the car, I feel a familiar energy start to build. The road stretches out before me, full of possibility and promise. But even as I merge onto the highway, my mind lingers on the rearview mirror, on what - and who - I'm leaving behind.

twenty-five
i miss you

Lauren

The house feels impossibly quiet after Dakota leaves. Even Roman, usually a bundle of energy this early in the morning, seems subdued, as if he can sense the shift in the air.

"Mommy," Roman's small voice breaks the silence as I'm pouring his cereal. "Where'd Dakota go?"

I freeze, the milk carton hovering over his bowl. We'd explained it to him this morning, but of course, at three years old, he might not have fully understood. I set the carton down and kneel beside his chair, meeting his confused gaze.

"Remember, sweetie? We talked about this. Dakota had to go away for work for a little while."

Roman's lower lip trembles slightly. "But he'll come back?"

"Of course he will," I assure him, smoothing his unruly hair. "He's just going to be gone for... for a long time."

"How long?" Roman persists, his little brow furrowed.

I hesitate. How do you explain three months to a toddler? "Remember when we counted the sleeps until your birthday? It's like that, but more sleeps."

Roman considers this, absently stirring his cereal. "Lots of sleeps," he echoes softly.

"That's right, baby. But we'll talk to him on the phone, and maybe even see him on the computer sometimes."

Roman nods, seeming to accept this explanation for now. But as I watch him eat his breakfast, his usual chatter replaced by thoughtful silence, I feel a pang of guilt. It's not just me who'll be missing Dakota these next few months.

Later in the afternoon as we're getting ready to leave for daycare, Roman suddenly runs to his room. He returns, clutching the stuffed dinosaur Dakota gave him for his birthday.

"Can I take Rex to daycare?" he asks, his eyes wide and pleading.

I feel my throat tighten with emotion. "Of course you can, sweetheart," I manage, helping him tuck Rex securely into his backpack.

As we head out the door, Roman's small hand in mine, I realize that navigating this separation isn't just about managing my own emotions. It's about helping Roman through it, too. Somehow, that makes it both harder and easier at the same time.

It's not until I'm back home that night after work,

the house silent, that the reality of Dakota's departure truly hits me. Three months. Ninety days of sleeping alone, of explaining to Roman why Dakota isn't here, of juggling everything on my own again.

Before I can spiral further, I reach for my phone. I need to talk to someone who gets it, who knows me. I need my best friend.

The phone rings three times before Shannon picks up, her voice bright despite the late hour. "Lauren! Hey, girl. How are you holding up?"

Just hearing her voice brings a rush of memories - giggling in the backseat of her mom's car on the way to high school, sneaking out to concerts, and crying on each other's shoulders over breakups. For a moment, I'm transported back to a time when Seattle was home, before LA, before Miles and Roman, before everything changed.

"He's gone," I say, my voice smaller than I'd like. "Dakota left for tour this morning."

"Oh, sweetie," Shannon's voice softens with sympathy. "I know that must be tough. How are you feeling?"

I close my eyes, trying to sort through the tangle of emotions in my chest. "Honestly? I don't know. Part of me is excited for him, you know? This tour is a big deal for the band. But another part..."

"Is terrified?" Shannon finishes for me.

"Yeah," I admit. "God, Shan, what if this is a mistake? What if he meets someone on the road, or decides this whole settled life isn't for him after all?"

"Lauren," Shannon's voice is firm now. "Stop. Dakota adores you and Roman. Anyone with eyes can see that."

I nod, even though she can't see me. "I know, I know. It's just... hard. And with school starting soon, and you being back in Seattle now..." I trail off, a familiar ache blooming in my chest at the thought of our hometown.

"Hey," Shannon says gently, seeming to sense where my mind has gone. "I know it's not easy for you to think about Seattle. Have you... have you talked to your parents at all?"

I feel my jaw clench involuntarily. "No," I say shortly. "And I don't plan to. They made their choices, and I made mine."

Shannon sighs, but doesn't push it. She knows better than anyone how deep that wound goes, how the disappointment of my parents when I told them I was keeping Roman still echoes in my nightmares.

"Well," she says after a moment, "I might be in Seattle, but I'm still here for you. Always. How about we set up a regular video chat? Maybe every Sunday?"

I feel a lump form in my throat, touched by her offer. "That would be amazing, Shan. Thank you."

The couch cushions envelop me as I sink down, the throw pillow I clutch to my chest still carrying a faint whiff of Dakota's scent. Outside, I can hear the familiar sounds of the neighborhood - cars driving by, and dogs barking. The world is moving on, oblivious to the ache in my chest.

"Of course," Shannon says slyly. "Now, tell me more

about this goodbye. Was it suitably romantic and steamy?"

I can't help but laugh, grateful for Shannon's ability to lighten the mood. As I launch into a slightly edited version of this morning's events, I feel some of the weight lift from my shoulders. Dakota may be gone, and Shannon may be in Seattle, but I'm not alone.

As I hang up with her, I feel a bit lighter. The ache of Dakota's absence is still there, but it's dulled somewhat by the promise of regular chats with my best friend.

I'm about to put my phone down when it buzzes in my hand. My heart skips a beat when I see Dakota's name on the screen.

> DAKOTA: At the venue for the show. Soundcheck was a shitshow. Missing you already. Give Roman a hug for me. x

A smile tugs at my lips even as I feel tears prick at my eyes. I type out a quick reply.

> ME: Miss you too. Roman took Rex to daycare to "remember you." Good luck with the show. Sorry about soundcheck. Can't wait to hear all about it later. xx

I set the phone down and take a deep breath. Three months suddenly feels both impossibly long and surprisingly manageable. One day at a time, I remind myself. One day at a time.

twenty-six
barely alive

Dakota

The roar of the crowd still echoes in my ears as I stumble off stage, sweat-soaked and grinning. Our set was tight, the energy electric. This is why I do this, why I love it.

I can still feel the vibration of my bass strings in my fingertips, the phantom weight of the instrument against my body. The last song, our new single *'Midnight Mirage,'* had the crowd going wild. I'd locked in with Emmett's drums, creating a groove so deep you could drown in it. When Brad's voice soared over Stefan's searing guitar solo, I saw people in the front row with tears in their eyes.

The guys are all whooping and high-fiving, riding the post-show high. Stefan's hair is plastered to his forehead, and his usually pristine white t-shirt is now translucent with sweat. Emmett's hands are shaking slightly - they always do after a particularly intense set - but his grin is a mile wide. And Brad, our normally cool and collected frontman, is bouncing on the balls of his feet like an excited kid.

"Did you hear them singing along?" Brad asks, his voice hoarse from belting out lyrics for the past hour. "Even to the new stuff. Fucking unreal, man."

I nod, still riding the wave of adrenaline. "That break-down in *'Fault Lines'* hit hard. I thought the floor was gonna cave in from all the jumping."

We're interrupted by our tour manager, reminding us we need to clear the side stage for Incendiary Ink. As we start helping to break down our gear, I can't help but smile. This feeling, this rush - it's better than any high I've ever known.

I reach for my phone, wanting to share this moment with Lauren. My fingers hover over the keys, trying to capture the rush in a text.

> ME: Show was amazing. Wish you could've been here. Miss you and Roman. x

Her reply comes quickly:

> LAUREN: So proud of you! Can't wait to hear all about it. Roman says hi. We miss you too. xx

A pang of longing hits me, but I push it aside. We've still got work to do.

The next hour is a blur of activity. We break down our equipment, pack up our gear, and do a quick meet-and-greet with some fans who won backstage passes. All the while, the muffled sounds of Incendiary Ink's set vibrate through the walls.

By the time we finish, I'm exhausted but still buzzing from the performance. We gather in our dressing room, sharing a few sodas and reliving the best moments of our set.

"Did you see that one girl in the front row? She knew every word!" Emmett exclaims, twirling a drumstick.

"Yeah, and what about when Brad almost ate it on that amp cable?" Stefan laughs, dodging a playful swipe from our lead singer.

I lean back, soaking it all in. This is what I've missed - the camaraderie, the shared excitement. For a moment, I almost forget the ache of missing Lauren and Roman.

Then, the building seems to shake with the thunderous applause, signaling the end of Incendiary Ink's set. A few minutes later, Chase, the lead singer, bursts into our dressing room, a bottle of champagne in each hand.

"Let's fucking celebrate, boys!" he shouts, popping one open and spraying it everywhere.

The room erupts in cheers. I hesitate, my sobriety a fragile thing in the face of such jubilation. But it's just one night, right? One drink to celebrate. I can handle that.

Chase thrusts a plastic cup of champagne into my hand, clapping me on the back. "To a killer first night!" he toasts.

I raise my cup with the others, the familiar scent of alcohol making my mouth water. It feels like it's been so long. *Just one*, I tell myself as I take a sip. The bubbles dance on my tongue, sharp and sweet.

For a split second, I'm transported back to another night, years ago. Chloe and I, celebrating some small victory I can't even remember now. The taste of cheap wine, her laughter, the feeling that everything was possible. Before it all went wrong.

I blink, and I'm back in the present. The taste of champagne turns bitter in my mouth, but I force myself to swallow. It's different now. I'm different. I can control it this time.

As I lower my cup, I catch Stefan's eye. His brow is furrowed, a question in his gaze. I give him a small nod, trying to convey that I've got this under control. He doesn't look convinced, but he turns away, engaging Chase in conversation.

Emmett is less subtle. He sidles up to me, keeping his voice low. "You sure about this, man? We can make excuses, head back to the hotel if you want."

I feel a flare of irritation. "I'm fine," I insist, taking another sip as if to prove my point. "It's one drink. To celebrate."

Emmett holds up his hands in surrender, but I can see the worry in his eyes. Even Brad, usually the life of the party, keeps glancing my way, his smile not quite reaching his eyes.

Their concern should be touching, but instead, it grates on me. I'm a grown man, for Christ's sake. I can handle one drink without completely falling off the wagon.

Can't I?

Chase, oblivious to the tension, throws an arm around my shoulders. "So, Dakota, you in for the after-party? There's this club down the street that's supposed to be insane."

I hesitate, feeling the weight of my bandmates' stares. Part of me wants to prove them wrong, to show them I can be around alcohol without losing control. Another part, the more rational part, knows I'm playing with fire.

But the champagne has already dulled that voice of reason, and Chase is looking at me expectantly. "Yeah," I hear myself say. "Yeah, I'm in."

As we file out of the dressing room, Stefan catches my arm. "Dakota," he starts, his voice low and serious.

I cut him off. "I said I'm fine. Drop it, okay?"

He looks like he wants to say more but just shakes his head and lets me pass. As we pile into Ubers, I catch a glimpse of my bandmates exchanging worried looks. I turn away, focusing instead on the excited chatter of the Incendiary Ink guys.

The Uber pulls away from the curb, and I lean my head against the cool glass of the window. The city lights blur past, and I feel a familiar buzz settling in my veins. It's been so long since I've felt this... normal. This free.

But with that freedom comes a nagging voice in the back of my head. What about Lauren? What about all the promises I've made?

I shake my head, trying to dislodge the thoughts. It's just one night. One celebration. I deserve this, don't I?

After all the hard work, all the struggles to stay sober. Surely, I've earned the right to let loose a little.

My phone buzzes in my pocket. Lauren. Guilt twists in my gut, but I silence it, shoving the phone deep into my pocket. *I'll call her tomorrow*, I promise myself. Right now, the night is young, and I've got something to prove.

To my bandmates, to myself, to the memory of Chloe that still haunts me. I can still hear her laughter from those nights long ago, a bittersweet reminder of everything I've lost and gained. I can do this. I can be normal. I can have just one drink.

Chase's voice cuts through my thoughts. "You're gonna love this place, Dakota. They've got this insane light show, and the drinks... man, the drinks are something else."

I nod, forcing a smile. "Sounds great," I say, ignoring the pit forming in my stomach. It's just one night.

As we pull up to the club, bass already thrumming through the car, a small voice in the back of my head whispers: *But will you stop at one?*

I drown it out with laughter at one of Chase's jokes as we tumble out of the car. The neon lights of the club beckon, promising escape, release. I follow the others inside, leaving my doubts on the curb behind me.

The club is a blur of strobe lights and pounding music. More drinks appear in my hand. I down them without thinking, chasing that euphoria, that freedom from thought.

A girl with purple hair presses against me on the dance floor. Her lips move, but I can't hear her over the music. She's pretty, I think distantly. But not as pretty as Lauren.

Lauren. The name cuts through the haze like a knife.

What the fuck am I doing?

I stumble away from Purple Hair, fumbling for my phone. The screen swims before my eyes, but I manage to pull up Lauren's contact. My finger hovers over the call button.

No. I can't let her hear me like this.

Instead, I text:

> ME: Miss yuo. Cant wait to com e
> home.

The typos mock me, a stark reminder of how far I've strayed in just one night. Shame burns through me, hotter than the alcohol in my veins.

I need to get out of here. I need to get back to the hotel. I need...

I need to be better than this.

As I push through the crowd towards the exit, I make a silent promise to Lauren, to Roman, to myself. This can't happen again. I won't let it.

But even as I think it, a traitorous part of me whispers: *Will you be able to keep that promise?*

The cool night air hits me like a slap as I stumble out of the club. My head spins, and I lean against the brick wall, trying to steady myself. The bass from inside still thrums through my body, a reminder of how close temptation remains.

I fumble again for my phone, squinting at the too-bright screen. It takes me three tries to successfully order an Uber. As I wait, I scroll through my contacts, thumb hovering again over Lauren's name. I want so badly to hear her voice. But what would I fucking say now? How could I explain this?

The Uber arrives mercifully quick. As I slide into the backseat, the driver eyes me warily in the rearview mirror. "Rough night?" he asks.

I nod, not trusting myself to speak. As we pull away from the curb, I watch the neon lights of the club recede. The guilt and shame sit heavy in my stomach, worse than any hangover.

Back at the hotel, I manage to make it to my room without running into any of my bandmates. Small fucking mercies. I collapse onto the bed, still fully clothed, the room spinning around me.

On the nightstand, my phone lights up with a text. Lauren.

> LAUREN: Hope you're having a great night! Can't wait to hear all about the show tomorrow. Love you. x

Fresh shame washes over me. I roll over, burying my face in the pillow. Tomorrow, I'll deal with this. Tomorrow, I'll be better. I have to be.

As I drift into an uneasy sleep, one thought echoes in my mind: *I can't let this happen again. I won't.*

But deep down, I'm terrified of how easy it was to fall.

No, I'm fucking petrified.

twenty-seven
why do i even try

Lauren

I check my watch for the third time in as many minutes. Dakota's supposed to call any second now. Roman's engrossed in his favorite cartoon, a bowl of apple slices within reach. I've got maybe an hour before he needs my attention again.

As I wait, I can't help but smile, remembering our last night together. Dakota's promises, his tender kisses, the way he held me like he never wanted to let go. It feels like a lifetime ago, even though it's been just a couple of weeks.

His touring has kept him busier than we'd planned, and our daily calls aren't daily anymore. Even texts are now few and far between, but I understand. I know how important this tour is for him and for the whole band. And from what I've seen online, they're killing it.

I've been looking forward to this call all day. I even put on a little makeup and Dakota's favorite shirt of mine

- the soft blue one he says brings out my eyes. It's not quite the same as having Dakota here, but it's something.

I answer the call with a bright smile, my heart doing a little flip as Dakota's face fills the screen. "Hey, you," I say. "I've been counting down the hours."

But the man on the screen doesn't match the Dakota in my mind. His hair is a mess, and there are dark circles under his eyes. He doesn't lean in close to the camera or give me that warm, crooked smile I've been dreaming about.

"Hey," he replies, his voice flat. "How's it going?"

My own smile falters. I'd prepared for this call, jotting down little anecdotes about Roman, questions about the tour, and ideas for staying connected. But faced with Dakota's apparent disinterest, all those plans crumble.

"We're... good," I say, trying to inject some enthusiasm into my voice. "How about you? How was last night's show? I've been dying to hear all about it."

Dakota shrugs, looking somewhere off-camera. "It was fine. Good energy."

I wait for more - for the detailed description of the crowd's reaction to their new song, for the funny story about a fan's sign that he'd usually share. But there's nothing.

Just silence.

"Oh," I say, scrambling to keep the conversation going. "Well, I wanted to tell you about my nursing school orientation. It's next week and—"

"Yeah, that's great, babe," he cuts in, clearly distracted. "Listen, we don't have a lot of time. The guys want to run through some new material before tonight's show."

The disappointment hits me like a physical blow. I'd cleared my schedule, prepared Roman, and even dressed up a little - all for a five-minute conversation with a distracted, distant version of the man I love.

As the call ends abruptly, I'm left staring at my reflection on the dark screen. The carefully applied makeup, the special shirt - they all seem ridiculous now. I'd prepared for a romantic moment across the miles, and instead got a harsh reminder of the reality of our situation.

The contrast between my expectations and the reality of the call leaves me feeling hollow. My heart feels like it's been stomped on. Is this what our relationship has become already? And if so, how will we survive entire months of this?

I don't know if I can do this.

"Mommy?" Roman's voice breaks through my thoughts. "Can I have more apples?"

I paste on a smile, pushing my worries aside. "Sure, baby. Let's get you some more."

As I cut up another apple for Roman, my mind races. Is this really how it's going to be? Dakota distant and irritable, and me left wondering what's really going on?

I want to believe in us, in what we're building. But as I watch Roman happily munching his apple slices, I can't help but wonder if love is enough when there's a whole country between us?

I shake my head, trying to dislodge the doubts. It's just one bad call. We'll figure it out. We have to.

Don't we?

Taking a deep breath, I reach for my phone again. I pull up my calendar, the neat rows of shifts at Sunny's interspersed with upcoming nursing school commitments. Structure. That's what I need right now.

I start adding new items: "Daily check-in with Dakota" goes into every evening slot. Even if it's just a quick text, we need to maintain that connection. "Self-care hour" gets penciled in twice a week - maybe I'll take a long bath or read a book that isn't a textbook for once.

"Mommy-Roman special time" goes in on Saturday mornings. I need to make sure he doesn't feel the strain of this situation. And "Shannon video chat" stays firmly in its Sunday evening spot. I'm going to need my best friend more than ever now.

As I finish, I feel a small sense of control returning. I can't change Dakota's behavior or the distance between us, but I can manage how I respond to it.

"Mommy, look!" Roman calls, proudly holding up his completed puzzle. "I did it all by myself!"

I smile, genuine this time. "That's amazing, baby! You're so smart."

Scooping him up in a hug, I make a silent promise to both of us. Whatever happens with Dakota, this is what is most important. I can't lose sight of that.

I may not have all the answers right now, but I've got love, determination, and a plan. It has to be enough.

For now, I push thoughts of Dakota aside and focus on Roman's chattering about his puzzle.

One day at a time, I remind myself. *One day at a time.*

twenty-eight
hopeless

Dakota

The harsh fluorescent lights of the gas station bathroom flicker as I splash cold water on my face. My reflection in the smudged mirror is a stranger – bloodshot eyes, unkempt beard, dark circles that no amount of stage makeup can hide. I've been on the road for a month, but I look like I've aged years.

"Hurry up, man!" Emmett's voice calls from outside. "Bus leaves in five!"

I grip the edges of the sink, trying to steady myself. The lingering effects of last night's drinks make the world tilt slightly. Or maybe that's just the guilt.

"Yeah, coming," I call back, my voice rough.

As I step out into the bright afternoon sun, squinting against the glare, I'm hit with a wave of déjà vu. Wasn't it just yesterday we were excited about gas station stops? Piling out of the tour bus, laughing and joking as we stocked up on snacks and stretched our legs?

Now, it's just another blur in a series of indistinguishable days and nights.

Brad eyes me as I climb back onto the bus. "You good?" he asks, concern evident in his voice.

I nod, not trusting myself to speak. I can feel the weight of the new flask in my jacket pocket, a constant reminder of how far I've fallen.

As the bus rumbles to life, I pull out my phone. Three missed calls from Lauren. Five unread messages. The sight of her name on the screen sends a jolt of shame through me.

I should call her back. I want to. But what would I say? How can I tell her that the man she loves, the one who promised to stay sober, is slowly drowning himself in alcohol and regret?

Instead, I put on my headphones and close my eyes, letting the motion of the bus lull me into a fitful sleep. In a few hours, we'll be at the next venue. Another show, another chance to lose myself in the music and the adoration of the crowd.

And after that? Well, there's always another drink waiting.

My fingers fumble over the strings as we launch into *'Midnight Mirage.'* The crowd doesn't seem to notice, but I catch Stefan's sharp glance. It's our new single, the one we're supposed to nail every night. Instead, I'm barely keeping up.

A month into the tour, and I'm already falling apart.

The rest of the set passes in a blur of bright lights and familiar chords. I'm running on autopilot, muscle memory carrying me through songs I could play in my sleep. Should be able to play in my sleep. The tremor in my hands is getting harder to ignore.

As we stumble off stage after the encore, I'm drenched in sweat and shaking slightly. The post-show high is already fading, leaving behind an achingly familiar emptiness.

"Dakota," Brad says, his tone serious. "We need to talk about what happened out there."

I force a laugh, reaching for a bottle of water. My hands shake as I unscrew the cap. "What do you mean? The crowd loved it."

"Yeah, they did," Stefan chimes in, "but you were off, man. That transition in *Midnight Mirage*—"

"I know, I know," I cut him off. "I'll nail it tomorrow. Just tired, you know? These late nights are catching up to me."

Emmett exchanges a look with Brad. "Maybe you should take it easy tonight. Get some rest."

I feel a flare of irritation. "I said I'm fine. Drop it, okay?"

Brad steps closer, lowering his voice. "Look, Dakota, we're worried about you. This isn't just about tonight. You've been off for weeks now. If you need help—"

"I don't need help," I snap, pushing past him. "I need some air."

I ignore their concerned looks as I head for the back

door. The cool night air hits me, and I take a deep breath.
My pocket feels heavy with the weight of the flask. I lean
against the building and light a cigarette, something else I
had recently quit and started again. Fuck it. Why not give
in to all my vices?

My phone buzzes. Lauren. Guilt twists in my gut as I
see the missed calls and unread messages. One catches
my eye.

> LAUREN: Two weeks into nursing
> school and I'm drowning in
> assignments. Could really use one of
> your pep talks right now. Miss you.
> When can we video chat?

I should call her back. I want to. God, I want to. But
how can I give her a pep talk when I can barely keep
myself together?

I take a swig from the flask, wincing at the burn. It's
been over a month of "just one more," turning into stumbling back to hotel rooms I barely remember. A month
of dodging Lauren's calls and making excuses about bad
reception or conflicting schedules.

Another text pops up.

> LAUREN: Roman asked about you
> again today. He misses his Dakota
> stories. We both do.

The words hit me like a physical blow. I promised
them both I'd stay connected, that I'd be there even from
a distance. Instead, I'm here, hiding in the shadows,

trying to numb myself to the reality of what I'm becoming.

After a while, my phone buzzes again. This time, it's not Lauren but a text from Chase. Fuck. How long have I been out here? I shake my flask and notice it's now empty. Shit.

> CHASE: Heading to a club downtown. You in?

I stare at the message, my thumb hovering over the reply button. I should say no. I should go back to the hotel, call Lauren, and try to salvage what's left of my sobriety and my relationship.

But the thought of facing the quiet of a hotel room, alone with my thoughts and the bone-gnawing need for another drink, is unbearable.

> ME: Yeah, I'm in. See you there.

As I pocket my phone and head towards the waiting Uber, I try to ignore the voice in my head telling me I'm making a mistake. It's drowned out by the promise of more alcohol, more numbing, more forgetting.

I'll call Lauren tomorrow, I promise myself. *I'll get it together. I'll be better.*

But even as I think it, I know it's a lie. The truth is, I'm losing control, and I don't know how to stop.

I don't know how to fucking stop.

twenty-nine
terrible things

Lauren

The dinner rush at Sunny's is in full swing, and I'm running on autopilot. Take orders, deliver food, refill coffee, repeat. It's mind-numbing work, but today, I'm grateful for it. It keeps me from dwelling on unanswered texts and missed video calls.

As I'm wiping down the counter, the bell above the door chimes. A blonde girl walks in, looking a little worse for wear. There's something vaguely familiar about her, but I can't quite place it.

"Welcome to Sunny's," I say, plastering on my customer service smile. "Sit anywhere you like."

She slides onto a stool at the counter, her eyes scanning the menu. When she looks up, there's a flash of recognition in her gaze.

"Lauren? Lauren Hudson?"

I blink, caught off guard. "Yes? I'm sorry, do I know you?"

She laughs, a brittle sound. "I guess you wouldn't

remember me. I'm Nikki. I used to date Miles back when he was with Earth Sign."

The name hits me like a slap. Miles. A flood of memories threatens to overwhelm me, but I push them back. I have customers to serve, and a job to do.

"Oh, right," I manage, my voice steadier than I feel. "What can I get you, Nikki?"

She orders a coffee and a burger, then leans forward, her eyes glittering with something that makes me uneasy. "So, how've you been? It's been what, three years since...?"

"Three years, two months," I reply automatically, then wince. I shouldn't still be counting.

Nikki nods, a knowing look on her face. "Yeah, it's rough. I heard about it through the grapevine. Such a shock, you know?"

I make a noncommittal noise, busying myself with pouring her coffee.

"I mean, who would've thought?" Nikki continues, seemingly oblivious to my discomfort. "Miles and that married chick. What was her name? Carly? Christie?"

My hand freezes mid-pour. "What?"

Nikki's eyes widen in mock surprise. "Oh shit, you didn't know? I thought... I mean, it was going around that Miles was seeing this married woman. Heard they died together. Overdose, right?"

The world tilts sideways. Miles... and a married woman? My mind races, pieces falling into place with sickening clarity. Dakota's wife, Chloe. The same night. The same way.

"I... I have to..." I stammer, barely aware of the coffee overflowing onto the counter.

"Lauren? You okay?" Nikki's voice sounds far away.

I nod mechanically, grabbing a rag to mop up the spilled coffee. "Fine. I'm fine. Your burger will be right up."

I escape to the kitchen, leaning against the cool metal of the refrigerator. My heart is pounding, my breath coming in short gasps.

It can't be true. It has to be a coincidence. Miles wouldn't...well, I can't say that. Miles would. But Chloe couldn't... could she?

But even as I try to deny it, I know. Deep down, I've always known there was more to the story of that night.

The order bell dings, jolting me back to reality. I have a shift to finish and customers to serve. But as I pick up Nikki's burger, my hands shaking slightly, one thought echoes in my mind:

I need to talk to Dakota. *Now.*

After delivering her food without a word, I fumble with my phone in the break room, my fingers shaking as I dial Dakota's number. Straight to voicemail. Again.

"Dakota, it's me. I... I need to talk to you. It's important. Please call me back as soon as you can."

I stare at the phone, willing it to ring. Nothing.

Taking a deep breath, I steel myself and head back out to the diner. Nikki's still at the counter, picking at her fries. I approach her, my heart pounding.

"Hey, Nikki," I say, trying to keep my voice casual. "I was wondering if we could talk a bit more. About Miles."

She looks up, surprise flickering across her face before settling into a knowing smirk. "Sure, honey. Pull up a chair. Looks like you could use a friendly ear."

I glance around the diner. It's quieted down, and my coworker nods that she can cover for me. I slide onto the stool next to Nikki.

"So," I begin, not sure where to start. "You mentioned Miles and... and this married woman."

Nikki nods, leaning in conspiratorially. "Yeah, it was the talk of the scene for a while. Miles always had a wandering eye, you know?"

The casual way she says it makes my stomach churn. "Did he... I mean, when you were together..."

"Oh honey," Nikki laughs, but there's no humor in it. "Miles cheated on everyone. It's just what he did. Hell, weren't you the other woman at one point?"

I feel my face flush. It's true. Miles and I had gotten together while he was still technically with someone else. I'd convinced myself it was different with us.

"But that was years ago," I protest weakly. "He was sober when we got serious. He wouldn't have..."

Nikki's expression softens slightly. "Look, Lauren, I'm not trying to hurt you. But Miles... he had demons. Being sober didn't change that. I was with him, too, when he got sober at one point. It never lasted. From what I heard, things started going south again when you got pregnant."

The words hit me hard. She's right. He did change then. I remember the mood swings, the late nights, the excuses. I'd chalked it up to nerves about becoming a father. The fighting had gotten so bad I had to move in with Shannon. Had I been that blind?

"Do you know anything about the woman he was with? The night he... the night it happened?" I ask, my voice barely above a whisper.

Nikki shrugs. "Not much. Just that she was married to some hotshot musician. Older than Miles. I think they met at a party or something."

Each word feels like another piece of a puzzle I never wanted to solve. Dakota's wife, Chloe. It had to be her.

"Lauren?" Nikki's voice breaks through my spiraling thoughts. "You okay? You look like you've seen a ghost."

I manage a weak smile. "I'm fine. Just... processing, I guess. Thanks for telling me all this."

As Nikki gathers her things to leave, she pauses. "For what it's worth, I think Miles really did love you. In his own fucked up way. He just... couldn't love himself, you know?"

I nod, not trusting myself to speak. As the bell chimes with Nikki's departure, I'm left sitting at the counter, my world completely tilted on its axis. Or is it just me that's about to fall off the planet?

My phone feels heavy in my pocket. Still no call from Dakota. But now, I'm not sure I want to hear what he might say. Because if Nikki's right, if Miles and Chloe really were together that night...

What does that mean for Dakota?

The lights of the police station buzz overhead as I shift from foot to foot, my backpack heavy with nursing text-books. I'm going to be late for class, but I can't walk away. Not now.

"I'm sorry, ma'am," the officer at the desk repeats, his voice tinged with impatience. "As I've explained, we can't release that information to you."

I lean forward, trying to keep my voice steady. "Please, I'm not just some random person. I was his girl-friend. I'm the mother of his child."

The officer's expression softens slightly, but he shakes his head. "I understand, but legally, you're not next of kin. Without a court order or permission from the imme-diate family, I can't give you access to that report."

"But it's been three years," I protest weakly. "Surely—"

"I'm sorry," he cuts me off, not unkindly. "Those are the rules. Is there anything else I can help you with?"

Defeated, I shake my head and turn away. As I push through the heavy glass doors, the morning sun feels too bright, too cheerful for the turmoil inside me.

I pull out my phone, thumb hovering over Dakota's name. Still no call back. Part of me wants to leave another message, to blurt out everything Nikki told me, to demand answers. But what if I'm wrong? What if it's all just a horrible coincidence?

No, I need to be sure before I say anything. But how?

As I walk to my car, my mind races. Miles' family? They barely spoke to him in those last few years, and they certainly don't talk to me now. Old bandmates? Maybe, but most of them fell out of touch after Miles died.

I slide into the driver's seat, resting my forehead against the steering wheel. The digital clock on the dashboard blinks at me, a reminder that I'm already ten minutes late for class.

With a sigh, I start the engine. For now, nursing school has to take priority. I've worked too hard to get here to throw it away on ghosts from the past.

But as I pull out of the parking lot, Nikki's words echo in my head. Miles and that married woman. Died together. The same night Dakota lost his wife.

It can't be a coincidence.

I merge onto the highway, my hands gripping the steering wheel too tightly. One way or another, I'm going to find out the truth. I have to.

For Roman. For myself.

And maybe, though it scares me to admit it, for Dakota, too.

thirty
heart of novocaine

Lauren

T he soft glow of my desk lamp casts long shadows across the living room. My nursing textbooks lie open, neglected, on the coffee table. The house creaks and settles around me, a reminder of its age and the life Shannon and I once had here. Now, it's just Roman and me... and sometimes Dakota.

I curl up on the worn couch, inhaling the familiar scent of chamomile tea. It reminds me of late nights with Dakota, his arm around me as we watched old TV shows. The mug's warmth seeps into my hands, a stark contrast to the cold dread in my stomach.

Shannon's face fills my laptop screen, her new Seattle apartment visible in the background. Despite the distance, we're still in the same time zone, the darkness outside her window mirroring my own.

"Lauren?" Shannon's voice cuts through my reverie. "You still there? You look like you've seen a ghost."

I force a weak smile. "Sorry, just... it's been a week. I can't focus on my studies, I can barely sleep..."

Shannon's brow furrows with concern. "Okay, spill it. What's going on?"

I take a deep breath, my eyes darting to the framed photo of Roman and Dakota on the mantel. "You remember Nikki? Miles' ex from way back?"

"Vaguely," Shannon nods. "Blonde, bit of a party girl? The one he was with before you?"

"That's her. She came into the diner a few days ago and... God, Shan, she told me something about Miles. About the night he died."

Shannon leans closer, her image pixelating slightly. "What? What did she say?"

The words stick in my throat, but I force them out. "She said... she said Miles was with someone that night. A married woman. That they... that they died together. And I told you Dakota's wife died the same night, right?"

"Holy shit," Shannon breathes. "Lauren, are you saying what I think you're saying? You think it was Dakota's wife?"

I nod, feeling tears sting in my eyes. "The timing fits. The circumstances. The hospital. It's too much of a coincidence, isn't it?"

Suddenly, I'm back in this very room, three years ago. The casual way I checked my phone that morning, expecting nothing more than a text from work. Instead, I got a voicemail from some guy I vaguely knew as Miles' friend. His words, hesitant and awkward: "Lauren, I... I think you should know. Miles died last night. Drug overdose."

I remember sinking onto this same couch, one hand on my swollen belly, feeling Roman kick as if he knew something was wrong.

"Lauren?" Shannon's voice pulls me back. "Where'd you go just now?"

I shake my head, wiping away a stray tear. "Just... remembering how I found out. God, Shan, what if I'd known then? What if..."

"Hey, no what-ifs," Shannon interrupts gently. "You can't change the past. But have you talked to Dakota about this?"

Guilt gnaws at me as I shake my head. "I tried calling him right away, but now I've been avoiding his calls. I don't know what to say, or how to even bring it up. What if I'm wrong, Shan? What if I'm just paranoid and seeing connections that aren't there?"

"And what if you're right?" Shannon counters. "Lauren, you can't sit on this. You need to talk to him."

"I know, I know. It's just..." I trail off, my eyes landing on Roman's latest artwork on the fridge. "I think we've built something good, you know? He's so great with Roman, and I... I love him. But this could change everything. This could really mess with his head right now. And I'm not sure he's in a great headspace as it is."

Shannon's quiet for a moment, her expression thoughtful. "Look, I get it. This is huge. But think about it - if it is true, don't you think Dakota deserves to know?

And if it's not, well, then you can put this whole thing to rest."

"There's more," I admit quietly. "I tried to get the police report, but they wouldn't give it to me. Said I wasn't next of kin."

"Of course they wouldn't," Shannon sighs. "But Dakota could get it, couldn't he? As Chloe's husband?"

"Yeah, I think so. But how do I even ask him to do that? 'Hey, honey, can you please check if your dead wife was cheating on you with my dead ex?'" The words taste bitter in my mouth.

"Start with the truth," Shannon suggests. "Tell him what Nikki said. Tell him your suspicions. Be honest about your fears."

I take a sip of my now-cold tea, letting Shannon's words sink in. "You're right. I know you're right. I just... I don't know how to have this conversation. And what if it changes how he feels about me? About Roman?"

"Lauren," Shannon's voice is firm. "That man adores you and Roman. This won't change that. But keeping secrets? That might."

As if on cue, I hear Roman stirring in his room. "Mommy?" his sleepy voice calls out.

"Just a sec, baby," I call back, then turn to Shannon. "I should go. But... thanks, Shan. I'll call him tomorrow. After my morning class."

"Good," Shannon smiles encouragingly. "And Lauren? Call me right after, okay? No matter how it goes."

"I will," I promise. "Thanks, Shan. I don't know what I'd do without you."

As I close my laptop, Roman pads into the living room, rubbing his eyes. "Mommy? Who were you talking to?"

"Just Aunt Shannon, sweetie," I say, pulling him onto my lap. "Did you have a bad dream?"

He nods, burying his face in my neck. "When's Dakota coming back?"

The innocent question feels like a punch to the heart. "Soon, baby. He's still working, remember?"

As I hold Roman close, my mind races. How will this affect him? Will it change the way Dakota looks at him? And what about nursing school? I've worked so hard to get here, but how can I focus on cellular biology when my past and present are colliding like this?

I carry Roman back to bed, tucking him in with Rex. As I smooth his hair, I make a silent promise. Whatever happens with Dakota, whatever the truth about Miles and Chloe turns out to be, I'll protect Roman. He's my priority, always. Miles' family might want nothing to do with us, just like my own parents, but that doesn't matter. We have each other.

But as I crawl into my own empty bed, doubt creeps in. Can Dakota and I survive this? What if this revelation changes everything we've built? What if 'together' isn't an option anymore?

Tomorrow, I tell myself. Tomorrow, I'll work up the courage to face this. I just hope we can face it together.

thirty-one
animals

Dakota

The whiskey burns as it slides down my throat, but it's not enough to dull the panic. Lauren's voicemail plays on repeat in my head: *"Dakota, it's me. I... I need to talk to you. It's important. Please call me back as soon as you can."*

That was days ago. I've called. I've texted. Nothing but radio silence.

My fingers shake as I dial her number again. One ring. Two. Three. I'm about to hang up when—

"Dakota?" Lauren's voice is hesitant, wary.

"Well, look who finally decided to pick up the fucking phone," I snarl, relief and rage and alcohol all warring for dominance. "Are you guys okay?"

"We're fine. But Dakota, I—"

"Wait, what? No, you don't get to talk," I interrupt, my voice rising. "Do you have any fucking idea what I've been going through? I thought something happened to you, or to Roman. I thought... I thought you were fucking leaving me or some shit."

"Dakota, please—"

"Please what? Please forgive you for fucking ignoring me for days? Please understand why you'd leave a cryptic voicemail and then disappear? What the fuck, Lauren?"

There's a pause, and when Lauren speaks again, her voice is tight. "Are you drunk?"

The question hits me like a slap, momentarily deflating my anger. "I... yeah. Yeah, I am. I'm sorry, Lauren. I'm so fucking sorry. I've been drinking again. I thought... something happened to you. And then I thought you were ghosting me. That I'd screwed everything up somehow."

"Dakota—" she starts, but now that I've begun, I can't stop.

"No, let me finish. I've been a mess. The tour, the pressure... I thought I could handle it. One fucking drink, you know? But it's never just one, is it? And then you called, and you sounded so serious, and then you wouldn't fucking answer, and I thought—"

"Dakota!" Lauren's sharp tone cuts through my rambling. "Stop. Just... stop. This isn't about you drinking. Well, it wasn't, but I guess we'll get to that."

I feel my stomach drop, anger giving way to fear. "What do you mean?"

She takes a deep breath. "Something's happened. Or... I found out something. About Miles. And... and your wife, Chloe."

The world seems to shift under me. "What about them?"

"I... A woman came into the diner. Nikki, Miles' ex. She told me... she said Miles was with a married woman the night he died. That they died together."

The words plow into me. I sink onto the edge of the hotel bed, my mind reeling. "What are you saying, Lauren?"

"I think... I think Miles and Chloe really were together that night, Dakota. The night they both died."

The silence stretches between us, heavy with implication. My drunk brain struggles to process this information. Miles and Chloe? Together?

"That's... that's fucking bullshit," I finally manage, anger flaring again. "You ignored me for days because of some gossip? Some bullshit story from Miles' ex?"

"It's not just gossip, Dakota," Lauren says, her own voice rising. "The timing fits. The circumstances. We talked about the coincidence--"

"Fuck the circumstances!" I shout. "Chloe wouldn't... she couldn't..."

But even as I say it, doubts creep in. The late nights. The secretive phone calls. The way she'd pull away when I tried to talk about starting a family. The sudden coldness in our last months together. I've been pretending this whole time that things were fine with us until the end, but I know deep down that I've been lying to myself.

"Dakota?" Lauren's voice is soft, uncertain. "I'm so

sorry. I didn't know how to tell you. I've been trying to figure out how to—"

"Is that why you've been ignoring my calls?" I interrupt, fury and hurt tangling in my chest. I have so many fucking emotions running through me at once, and I don't know where to direct any of it. "You've known this for days, and you didn't fucking tell me? You let me think the worst?"

"I was trying to process it myself," Lauren shoots back. "I even tried to get the police report, but they wouldn't give it to me. Said I wasn't next of kin."

Her words barely register as my mind spirals. Chloe. My wife. The woman I'd promised to love and cherish. Had she really betrayed me like this? Had our entire marriage been a lie?

"Dakota, are you still there?" Lauren's voice cuts through my thoughts.

"Yeah," I manage, my voice hoarse. "I just... I can't fucking believe it. Chloe and I, we had our problems, sure, but this? Cheating on me with your ex? Fucking dying with him? It's too much."

"I know it's a lot to take in," Lauren says softly. "I'm so sorry, Dakota. I never wanted to hurt you like this."

A bitter laugh escapes me. "Hurt me? Lauren, if this is true... God, my whole life with Chloe feels like a fucking lie now. Every memory, every moment... was she thinking of him? Was I just a placeholder?"

"Dakota, you can't think like that—"

"How else am I supposed to think?" I snap, anger

rising again. "My dead wife might have been cheating on me with your dead ex. It's like some sick fucking cosmic joke."

There's a pause, and when Lauren speaks again, her voice is thick with unshed tears. "I don't know what to say, Dakota. I don't know how to make this better."

The fight drains out of me, leaving nothing but a hollow ache. "You can't make it better, Lauren. No one can."

We sit in silence, miles apart but connected by this shared pain. Finally, I clear my throat. "I need to... I need some time to think. To sober up. Can we... can we talk tomorrow? When I'm clear-headed?"

"Yeah," Lauren agrees softly. "That's probably a good idea. Dakota?"

"Yeah?"

"I do love you. Whatever this means, whatever happens... I love you."

The words are both a balm and a knife. "I love you too," I whisper, feeling utterly lost.

As the call ends, I stare at the bottle of whiskey on the nightstand. The guilt and shame of my harsh words with Lauren slice deep into my soul. I was a fucking dick to her, but yet she still said she loved me. What the fuck is wrong with me? How could I do that to her? She didn't deserve any of that. Fuck, she's probably going through more pain than I am right now, and I just completely ignored her feelings.

This has to fucking stop.

With a sudden surge of resolve, I grab the bottle and head for the bathroom. As I watch the amber liquid swirl down the drain, one thought echoes in my mind:

What the hell do I do now? And how do I even begin to unravel the truth about Chloe?

thirty-two
in the air tonight

Lauren

I set my phone down on the coffee table, my hand trembling. The echo of Dakota's voice - slurred, angry, then broken - still rings in my ears. My chest tightens, each breath a conscious effort. The faint scent of Dakota's cologne on the throw blanket, once comforting, now makes my stomach turn.

He's drinking again. The suspicion I've been pushing away is now a cold, hard fact. The mood swings, the missed calls, the way his voice would change as our conversations went on - it all makes sense now. But is that all he's doing? Everything is now in question.

I stand abruptly, needing to move. The floor creaks under my feet as I pace, a sound that usually irritates me but now grounds me in reality. My eyes dart around the room, landing on the framed photo of Roman and Dakota on the mantel. Dakota's smile is wide and genuine, and he helps Roman build a tower of blocks. The sight sends a fresh wave of nausea through me.

How did we get here? Just a few months ago, everything seemed so perfect. Dakota was sober, we were happy, and even the prospect of his tour couldn't dampen our spirits. Now? Now, I'm not sure of anything.

A memory surfaces: the day I found out I was pregnant with Roman. The mix of doubt and joy, fear and hope. The argument with Miles ended with him leaving to get drunk or high. When Miles died, I'd promised myself that my child would never know the pain of loving an addict.

"Not again," I whisper to the empty room. "I can't put Roman through this."

But even as I think it, Dakota's face swims in my mind. His gentle way with Roman, and his support of my nursing school dreams. Is it fair to compare him to Miles?

I move to the kitchen, my hands shaking as I fill a glass with water. My nursing textbooks are spread across the table, and mock exams and study guides are a stark reminder of the life I'm trying to build. The upcoming pharmacology test seems trivial now, but I know it's crucial for my future.

Sipping the water, I lean against the counter, my mind racing. On top of everything else, the financial juggling act I've been performing suddenly feels even more precarious. I've prided myself on managing everything on my own - the rent, the daycare fees, the nursing program expenses. I even turned down Dakota's offers to help. But now, the weight of it all feels crushing. It's not about the money Dakota could provide; it's about the emotional support, the partnership I thought we were building. Can I really handle all of this - single motherhood, a demanding nursing program, and now this emotional turmoil - entirely on my own?

A soft sound from Roman's room makes me look up. I tiptoe to his door, peering in. He's sleeping peacefully, Rex the dinosaur clutched to his chest. The sight of him, so innocent and unaware, brings tears to my eyes.

"I have to protect you," I whisper. "No matter what."

Back in the living room, I curl up on the couch, hugging a pillow to my own chest. I should be reviewing my notes for tomorrow's class, but instead, my mind conjures images of Dakota on tour - in bars, backstage parties, and hotel rooms with mini-bars. I shake my head, trying to dispel the thoughts.

What if he gets help? A small voice in my head argues. *What if this was just a slip-up?*

But another voice, louder and more insistent, reminds me of the stories Miles told me about his struggles with addiction. The constant battle, the relapses, the toll it took on everyone around him. Hell, then he flat-out showed me what it's like.

I reach for my phone again, my thumb hovering over Shannon's number. She told me to call her after I spoke to Dakota, but what would I even say? How do I explain that in trying to uncover one painful truth, I stumbled upon another?

Instead, I open my calendar app. Classes, study groups, Roman's daycare schedule - the neat rows of commitments stare back at me. How am I supposed to focus on any of this when my personal life is in such chaos?

I force myself to consider the possibilities. If I end things with Dakota now, I'll be hurt, but I'll protect Roman and myself from potential future pain. If I stay, I'm opening myself up to a world of uncertainty. Can I handle the stress of nursing school, single motherhood, AND a partner struggling with addiction?

But then I think about Dakota's laugh and the way he looks at me sometimes, like I'm the only person in the world. The way Roman's face lights up when he sees him. Can I really walk away from that?

As I finally drag myself to bed, exhaustion settling into my bones, one thought keeps circling in my mind: Is love enough when history seems determined to repeat itself? And more importantly, am I strong enough to find out?

I set my alarm, knowing sleep will be elusive tonight. Tomorrow, Dakota will call when he's sober. Tomorrow, I'll have to start making decisions.

For now, I close my eyes and try to quiet my mind, the weight of the future heavy on my chest.

thirty-three
adrenaline

Dakota

The pounding on my hotel room door slices through my skull like a jackhammer. I groan, rolling over in sheets damp with night sweats. The digital clock on the nightstand blinks an accusing 1:47 PM. Shit.

"Dakota! Open up, man. We're worried about you."

Brad's voice, muffled through the door, is tinged with concern. I drag myself out of bed, the room spinning slightly as I stand. The taste in my mouth is foul, a reminder of last night's poor decisions.

I crack open the door, wincing at the harsh hallway light. Brad's worried face swims into focus.

"Jesus, Dakota. You look like hell."

"Feel like it, too," I mutter, stepping aside to let him in. The room reeks of stale booze and desperation.

Brad's eyes scan the chaos - empty mini bottles scattered across the floor, my bass propped haphazardly in a corner, papers strewn across the desk. His gaze lands on the crumpled photo of Chloe I'd pulled from my wallet last night in a moment of drunken nostalgia.

"Want to tell me what's going on?" he asks softly. "You missed soundcheck, and you're not answering your phone. Stefan and Emmett are freaking out, and Ian's about to have a fucking heart attack."

I collapse onto the bed, rubbing my face. The mention of the band sends a fresh wave of guilt through me. "It's... it's complicated, Brad. I fucked up. I've been drinking again."

"No shit, Sherlock," Brad nods, unsurprised. He sits down in the desk chair, leaning forward. "Talk to me, man. What's really going on?"

For a moment, I consider brushing him off. But the weight of everything suddenly feels too heavy to bear alone. "It's Chloe," I start, my voice cracking. "I found out... I think she was cheating on me with Lauren's ex, Miles. We think they might've died together, Brad. They died the same fucking night."

As I say the words, a memory flashes unbidden - Chloe, laughing in our kitchen, flour on her cheek as she tried to bake cookies. She'd looked so happy, so alive. Had she been thinking of him even then?

Brad's sharp intake of breath brings me back to the present. "Holy shit. Are you sure?"

I shake my head, feeling the ache behind my eyes intensify. "Not completely. But there's too many coincidences. I need to know for sure. I need to see the police report."

"The police report?" Brad echoes, brow furrowed.

"Yeah. Lauren tried to get it, but they wouldn't give it to her. But I'm Chloe's husband - *was* her husband. They'll have to give it to me, right?"

Brad nods slowly. "Probably, yeah. But Dakota, are you sure you want to go down this road? Digging into the past like this... it might do more harm than good."

Another memory surfaces - Lauren's smile the first time I met her at the diner, the way her eyes crinkled at the corners. The warmth I'd felt was the first spark of hope after years of numbing grief. What would this do to us?

"I have to fucking know, Brad," I insist, the words tasting bitter in my mouth. "I can't... I can't move forward with Lauren, with anything, until I know the truth."

Brad's quiet for a moment, then stands up. "Alright. If that's what you need to do, I'll help you if I can. But first, you need to shower and eat something. And then we need to talk about the drinking."

I wince, but nod. He's right, of course.

"I'll do some research, see what we need to do to get that report," Brad continues. "You get yourself together. And Dakota? We're going to figure this out. All of it. You're not alone in this, okay?"

For the first time in I don't know how long, I feel a glimmer of hope. "Thanks, man. I mean it."

As Brad leaves to make some calls, I force myself into the shower. The hot water sluices over me, washing away the physical evidence of my bender, if not the emotional toll. By the time I'm dressed in clean clothes, I feel almost human again.

The room seems smaller now, closing in on me. Through the thin walls, I can hear the muffled sounds of a neighboring TV, the distant hum of an ice machine - the mundane soundtrack of tour life that usually fades into the background. Today, each sound grates on my nerves.

Brad returns, a serious look on his face. "Okay, I've got some information. Good news is, you can get the report. Bad news is, we're halfway across the country. You'll need to request it by mail and have someone pick it up for you in person back in LA."

I nod, disappointment mixing with determination. "Alright. Let's start the mail request. And maybe... maybe I can ask Lauren if she knows anyone who could pick it up faster?"

"Are you sure you want to involve Lauren in this?" Brad asks cautiously.

I run a hand through my damp hair, conflicted. Lauren's face flashes in my mind again, this time tinged with worry. The way she'd sounded during our last call, concern etched in her voice. She knows now that I've been drinking. "I don't know, man. But she's already involved, isn't she? She's the one who told me about all this."

Brad nods thoughtfully. "Fair point. Just... be careful, Dakota. This is heavy stuff."

"I know," I sigh, the weight of it all settling back on my shoulders. "Believe me, I know."

As Brad outlines the next steps - starting the mail request, looking into AA meetings, or phone counseling options, and preparing for tonight's show - I find myself staring at my reflection in the mirror. The man looking back at me seems older, worn. But beneath the exhaustion, I see a flicker of the old Dakota - the one who fell in love with music, the one who promised Lauren a future.

I have to do this, I realize. Not just for me, but for all of us - the ghost of Chloe, the memory of Miles, the future with Lauren and Roman I'm desperate to salvage. I have to face this demon, slay this dragon, whatever it takes.

As Brad leaves to rejoin the others, I pick up my bass, fingers finding familiar chords. The music has always been my sanctuary, my way of processing the world. Maybe it can help me navigate this storm, too.

I check my phone one last time. Lauren's missed call stares back at me. I'll call her back soon, I decide. After I've started the process for the police report, after I've found my footing again. I can't avoid the repercussions of our call last night forever.

For now, I've got a mystery to solve and a demon to face. The road ahead is long and treacherous, but for the first time in a while, I don't feel like I'm walking it alone. It's time to face the music - in every sense of the phrase.

thirty-four
i feel it too

Lauren

The kitchen light above me flickers, matching the erratic rhythm of my thoughts. It's 7:17 PM, and still no call from Dakota. My phone sits silent on the counter, a constant reminder of the void where his voice should be.

I run my fingers over the smooth, cool surface of my pharmacology textbook, but the words blur before my eyes. Instead, my mind replays Dakota's slurred words from yesterday, the anger and pain in his voice mixing with older, more painful memories.

Suddenly, I'm back in our old apartment, the one Miles and I shared. The sour smell of stale beer and unwashed clothes. Miles, sprawled on the couch, empty bottles at his feet. His bloodshot eyes were unfocused and accusing. "You don't understand," he'd slurred. "I need it."

I shake my head, Dakota isn't Miles, I remind myself. But the knot in my stomach tightens all the same.

"Mommy?" Roman's small voice breaks through my reverie. He stands in the doorway, clutching Rex the dinosaur. "Can we have a snack?"

I paste on a smile, pushing away my worries. "Sure, baby. How about some apple slices?"

As I cut the apple, I watch Roman settle at the table, his little legs swinging. He picks up one of my highlighters, mimicking my study habits by drawing yellow lines across his coloring book.

"Is Dakota coming back soon?" he asks, eyes on his 'homework.'

The knife slips, nearly nicking my finger. "No, sweetie. Dakota's very busy with his music right now. He's all the way in another state."

Roman nods, accepting this with the easy faith of a child. But I can't help wondering, what if Dakota's drinking escalates? What if Roman starts to notice the mood swings, the broken promises? The thought makes me feel sick.

I can't take it anymore. I need to talk to someone who understands.

Leaving Roman with his snack and homework, I step into the living room and dial Shannon's number. She picks up on the second ring.

"Lauren? Is everything okay?"

I let out a shaky breath, sinking onto the couch. "Not really. I... Dakota's drinking again."

There's a pause on the other end of the line. "Oh, honey. Are you sure?"

"Yes," I say, my voice barely above a whisper. "When

we talked yesterday, he even admitted it. And now he's not returning my calls."

"Shit," Shannon breathes. "I'm so sorry, Lauren. What happened? Did he say anything specific?"

I close my eyes, remembering. "It was about that thing I told you... about Miles and Chloe. He was angry and confused. But it wasn't just that. His words were slurred, and his mood was all over the place. It was like... like talking to Miles on a bad night."

"Oh, Lauren," Shannon's voice is soft and sympathetic. "That must have been so hard for you."

"It was," I admit, feeling tears prick in my eyes. "And now, with the silence... I can't help but think he's spiraling. And I don't know what to do."

"What do you want to do?" Shannon asks gently.

I let out a bitter laugh. "Run? Hide? Pretend none of this is happening?" I pause, taking a shaky breath. "I don't know. Part of me wants to be there for him, to help him through this. But another part..."

"Is terrified of going through it all again," Shannon finishes for me.

"Exactly," I whisper. "I swore after Miles that I'd never get involved with another addict. That I'd never put Roman through that. And now..."

"Hey," Shannon's voice is firm but kind. "Dakota isn't Miles. You can't compare them."

"Can't I?" I ask, standing up to pace the room. "The drinking, the mood swings, the unreliability. It's all so familiar. I really thought he was different. He was so good with Roman, so supportive of my school. But now... God, what was I thinking?"

"You were thinking that you found someone who made you happy," Shannon says softly. "There's nothing wrong with that."

I shake my head, even though she can't see me. "But at what cost? I can't put Roman through this. I can't go through it myself. Not again."

"So, what are you saying?" she asks. "Are you thinking of ending things with Dakota?"

The question stops me in my tracks. "I... I don't know," I admit, my voice barely audible. "Part of me wants to run as far and fast as I can. But another part..."

"Still loves him," Shannon finishes for me.

"Yeah," I whisper, feeling the tears start to fall. "God, why is this so hard?"

"Because love is complicated," she says. "And addiction is a bitch. But Lauren, you need to remember something."

"What's that?"

"You're stronger now than you were with Miles. You've been through this before. You know the signs, and you know your worth. Whatever you decide to do, you'll be okay. You and Roman both."

I sink back onto the couch, letting her words wash over me. "But what if I'm overreacting? What if this was just a slip?"

"Does it feel like a slip?" Shannon asks.

I think about the missed calls, and the erratic

behavior over the past few weeks. "No," I admit. "It feels like the beginning of something bigger."

"Then trust your instincts," Shannon advises. "You've been here before. You know what to look for."

"But what do I do?" I ask, feeling lost. "Do I confront him? Just... end it before it gets worse?"

"I can't make that decision for you, honey," Shannon says gently. "But I think you need to ask yourself some hard questions. Can you handle being with someone in active addiction? Are you willing to go through that journey with Dakota if he decides to get help? And most importantly, what's best for you and Roman?"

I nod, even though she can't see me. "You're right. I know you're right. It's just... I thought we had a future, you know? I could see it so clearly."

"I know," Shannon's voice is soft with understanding. "But remember, Lauren. Your future isn't dependent on Dakota or any man. You're building an amazing life for yourself and Roman. Don't lose sight of that."

Her words hit me hard, a reminder of everything I've worked for. "Thanks, Shan. I don't know what I'd do without you."

"Anytime, babe. That's what I'm here for. And Lauren? Whatever you decide, I've got you. Always."

After we hang up, I sit in the quiet of the living room, Shannon's words echoing in my mind. She's right - I am stronger now. But is strength enough to weather this storm?

My reflection in the glass looks tired, worried. But behind me, I can see more of my nursing textbooks spread across the coffee table, a reminder of the future I'm building. A future that, until yesterday, I thought included Dakota.

Now, I'm not so sure.

"Mommy?" Roman calls from the kitchen. "Can you help me with my homework?"

Reality crashes back in. I have responsibilities. A life to lead, with or without Dakota in it. I can't put everything on hold waiting for him to call.

With a deep breath, I turn away from the window. "Coming, sweetie."

As I sit next to Roman, helping him color within the lines, I make a silent promise to myself. Whatever happens with Dakota, I'll face it. I'll be strong - for Roman, for my future, for myself.

The rest will have to wait. For now, this moment with my son is what matters most.

thirty-five
the jester

Dakota

The stale air of the hotel room presses down on me, still heavy with the scent of yesterday's whiskey and regret. Outside, I can hear the distant rumble of the tour buses being loaded, a reminder of the relentless pace of life on the road. My fingers shake slightly as I scroll to Lauren's number, the bright screen a stark contrast to the dimness of the room.

I've been putting this off for hours, torn between the desperate need to hear her voice and the fear of what she might say. The memory of our last conversation, my words slurred and angry, plays on repeat in my mind. God, what must she think of me?

Taking a deep breath, I hit dial. Each ring sends a jolt of anxiety through my body.

"Dakota?" Lauren's voice is hesitant and guarded. The warmth that usually colors her tone when she says my name is noticeably absent.

"Hey," I say, my own voice rougher than I expected. I

clear my throat, trying to shake off the remnants of last night's cigarettes. "I... I'm sorry I didn't call back sooner. Things have been..."

"Complicated?" she finishes for me, her tone flat.

I wince, pacing the small space between the bed and the window. "Yeah. Look, Lauren, about the other day-"

"You were drunk," she interrupts, cutting straight to the chase.

The bluntness of her statement catches me off guard. My free hand instinctively goes to the back of my neck, a nervous habit I thought I'd kicked years ago. "I... yes. I was. I'm sorry, I-"

"How long has this been going on, Dakota?" The pain in her voice is palpable, and it cuts deeper than any hangover.

I sink onto the edge of the bed, shame washing over me. "It started after the first show. I thought I could handle just one drink, but..."

"The first freaking show? It's never just one, is it?" The bitterness in her tone makes me flinch.

A memory flashes unbidden - the electrifying high of that first show, the champagne flowing freely backstage. I'd felt invincible that night, on top of the world. How quickly it all came crashing down.

"Lauren, I'm sorry. I know I messed up. But I'm going to fix this. I'm going to meetings, I'm talking to Brad-"

"Stop," she says, and the weariness in her voice makes my heart sink. "Just... stop, Dakota. I've heard all this before."

"What do you mean?"

There's a long pause. When Lauren speaks again, her voice is barely above a whisper. "With Miles. I've heard all these promises before. The *'I'm sorries,'* the *'I'll do betters.'* And I just... I can't do it again."

Her words hit me sideways. The room seems to tilt, and I grip the edge of the bed to steady myself. "Lauren, please. I'm not Miles. This isn't the same-"

"Isn't it?" she cuts me off. "The drinking, the mood swings, the unreliability. It all feels pretty familiar from where I'm standing."

I feel panic rising in my chest, making it hard to breathe. "Lauren, I love you. I love Roman. I don't want to lose you."

"I don't want to lose you either," she says softly. "But I have to think about Roman. I have to think about myself. I can't go through this again."

"What are you saying?" I ask, though I'm absolutely terrified of the answer.

Another long pause. I can almost see her biting her lower lip the way she does when she's trying not to cry. "I'm saying... I think I need some time, Dakota. To think. To figure out if I can do this. If we can do this."

No, no, no.

I stand up abruptly, needing to move, to do something. "Lauren, please. We can work through this. I'll do whatever it takes."

"I've heard that before, too," she says, and I can hear the tears in her voice now. "I'm sorry, Dakota. I just... I need some time."

"Wait," I say, desperation coloring my voice. "What about... what about Miles and Chloe? Don't you think we need to figure that out together?"

Her sharp intake of breath is audible even through the phone. "Dakota... I can't deal with that right now. Not when I'm not sure I can trust you not to go off the deep end with whatever we find out. I'm sorry, but I need time."

Before I can respond, she ends the call. I stare at the phone in disbelief, my mind reeling. This can't be happening. Not now. Not when I need her most.

The mini-bar catches my eye, its contents promising a temporary escape from this nightmare. For a moment, the urge to lose myself in a bottle is overwhelming. But I resist, my knuckles turning white as I grip the phone tighter. If there's any hope of salvaging things with Lauren, I have to stay sober.

A knock at the door startles me. "Dakota?" Brad's voice calls out. "Soundcheck in 10, man."

Right. The show. The tour. Life goes on, even as mine feels like it's falling apart.

"Be right there," I call back, my voice sounding strange to my own ears.

As I grab my bass, I catch a glimpse of myself in the mirror. Something I've been doing a lot of lately – looking for the flaws. The man staring back at me looks lost, broken. But beneath the pain and fear, I see a flicker of determination.

I will fix this. Somehow, some way, I will make this right. For Lauren, for Roman, for myself.

Because the alternative - a life without them - is too painful to bear.

———

The backstage area is a cacophony of sound and motion. Roadies rush past, breaking down equipment. The air is thick with the smell of sweat, undercut by the faint scent of spilled beer. My shirt clings to my back, damp from the heat of the stage lights, and my fingers ache pleasantly from an hour of playing.

"Killer set, man," Chase from Incendiary Ink materializes beside me, his energy seemingly unaffected by the grueling schedule. "You guys really brought it tonight."

I manage a weak smile. "Thanks. You guys were amazing, too."

Chase grins, slinging an arm around my shoulders. The scent of his cologne mingles with the ever-present smell of alcohol that seems to follow him. "We're heading to this strip club downtown. You in? First round's on me."

The offer hangs in the air, tempting and dangerous. A familiar warmth spreads through my chest at the thought of that first drink, the way it would take the edge off, make everything a little easier to bear. For a moment, I'm back at that first after-party, the taste of expensive champagne on my tongue, the world soft and warm around the edges.

I shake my head, dispelling the memory. "Thanks, but... I think I'm gonna pass tonight."

Chase's eyebrows shoot up in surprise. "Seriously? Come on, man, it's gonna be epic."

From across the room, I see Brad watching our inter-action, his expression a mix of concern and hope. Stefan and Emmett are helping to pack up their gear, but I can tell they're listening too.

I take a deep breath, steeling myself. "I'm sure it will be. I just... I can't. Not tonight."

Mark, Incendiary Ink's guitarist, steps closer, his eyes narrowing. "Everything okay, Dakota? You've seemed off lately."

For a moment, I consider brushing it off, making up some excuse. But I'm tired of lying, tired of hiding. "Actually, no. Everything's not okay. I'm... I'm trying to stay sober."

The backstage area suddenly feels too quiet, too still. Chase and Mark exchange a look I can't quite decipher. From the corner of my eye, I see Brad give me a subtle nod of approval.

"Shit, man," Chase says finally. "That's rough. Respect for being upfront about it. This industry can be a bitch for staying clean."

Mark nods slowly. "Yeah, the constant parties, the stress... it's not easy. And I'm sure we haven't been helping with that." He gives Chase a sideways glance. "You got support?"

I think about the AA app I downloaded earlier, and the meetings I've been researching. "I'm working on it," I say, surprised by the determination in my voice. "One day at a time, right?"

Chase squeezes my shoulder. "That's the way. If you need anything..."

"Thanks," I say, feeling a lump form in my throat. "I appreciate it."

As they head out, Chase turns back. "You sure you don't want to come? We could do something non-alcoholic, hit up a diner or something?"

The offer is tempting, but I shake my head. My hands are already starting to shake slightly, my body craving what I'm denying it. "Not tonight. But... maybe next time?"

Chase grins. "I'll hold you to that. Take care of yourself, Dakota."

As I watch them leave, I feel a mix of longing and relief. The urge to follow them, to lose myself in the night, is almost overwhelming. But I stand my ground.

Brad approaches, his voice low. "Proud of you, man. That couldn't have been easy."

I nod, not trusting myself to speak. He seems to understand, giving my shoulder a quick squeeze before heading off to help with the gear.

Back in the dressing room, I ignore the mini-bar and grab my laptop instead. As I start researching local AA meetings for our next stop, I can't help but wonder: *Can I really do this? Stay sober on tour, with temptation around every corner?*

I don't have all the answers. But for tonight, I made the right choice. And maybe, just maybe, that's enough for now.

thirty-six
the unknown

Lauren

My eyes burn from hours of studying my pharmacology textbook, and the faint aroma of stale coffee clings to my clothes. I roll my shoulders, trying to ease the tension that's built up over the past four hours of cramming.

ACE inhibitors, beta-blockers, calcium channel blockers... The words swim before my eyes, a jumble of medical jargon that could make or break my nursing school career. Tomorrow's exam looms large – three hours of grueling multiple-choice questions and case studies that will test everything we've learned about cardiovascular pharmacology this semester.

But instead of focusing on the difference between lisinopril and metoprolol, my mind keeps drifting to Dakota. I check my phone again, the screen's blue light harsh in the dimness of the library carrel. Still no message.

It's been days since our last conversation. Days of silence that I asked for.

And I hate it.

I close my eyes, and unbidden, a memory surfaces: Dakota, laughing as he tries to teach Roman how to play air guitar. The joy on both their faces, the easy comfort between them. My chest tightens at the thought of losing that, of Roman losing that.

But then another image intrudes – Miles, passed out in the apartment's parking lot, an empty bottle in his hand. The fear, the uncertainty, the constant walking on eggshells. Can I risk putting Roman through that again?

"You okay?" Sonya's voice breaks through my reverie. She's standing at the end of my carrel, concern etched on her face. "You look like you're a million miles away."

I force a smile. "Just stressed about the exam. You know, the usual pre-test jitters."

Sonya nods sympathetically. "Tell me about it. I'm still not sure I understand the differences in beta-blocker selectivity. Want to do a quick review?"

For a moment, I'm tempted to say yes, to lose myself in the familiar rhythm of study. But the weight of everything – Dakota, Miles, Chloe, the exam – suddenly feels overwhelming.

"Thanks, but I think I need some air," I say, gathering my things. "Good luck with your studying."

Outside, the cool night air is a shock to my system after hours in the stuffy library. I breathe deeply, trying to clear my head. The campus is quiet at this late hour, just a few students hurrying between buildings, their faces illuminated by the glow of their phones.

I pull out my own phone, thumb hovering over Dakota's name. Should I call him? What would I even say?

'Hey, I know you're struggling with sobriety, and I dropped a bomb about your dead wife potentially cheating on you, and I said I needed space, but I wanted to hear your voice?'

I let out a bitter laugh, startling a nearby squirrel.

The truth is, I want to call him. I want to hear his voice, to know he's okay. But I'm also terrified of what I might hear – slurred words, broken promises, the sound of his world falling apart.

And then there's the other nagging thought, the one I've been trying to push away: *Miles and Chloe*. The coincidence of their deaths, the possibility that they were together... it's like a puzzle with mismatched pieces, and I can't stop trying to fit them together.

But should I? Do I really want to uncover a truth that could potentially destroy everything?

I sink onto a nearby bench, suddenly exhausted. The cool metal seeps through my jeans, grounding me in the present.

I have an exam in less than ten hours. An exam that could determine the course of my future, and my ability to provide for Roman. I can't let my personal life derail everything I've worked for.

And yet...

I pull up the photo of Dakota and Roman building a

pillow fort in the living room. Their smiles, so genuine and carefree, make my heart ache. This is what I'm fighting for, I realize. Not just a degree, not just a better future, but the chance at a family, at happiness.

But at what cost?

With a deep breath, I put my phone away and pull out my flashcards, squinting at them in the low light of a nearby post. Beta-blockers, ACE inhibitors, calcium channel blockers... I can do this. I have to.

As for Dakota, Miles, Chloe, and all the unanswered questions... they'll have to wait. At least for tonight.

But as I force myself to focus on pharmacology, I can't shake the feeling that everything is about to change. For better or worse, I'm not sure.

All I know is that when the dust settles, I need to be standing – for myself, for Roman, and maybe, just maybe, for Dakota, too.

The scratch of pencils on paper fills the air, punctuated by the occasional cough or shuffle of feet. The exam room smells of anxiety and cheap floor cleaner, a combination that turns my stomach. I shift in my hard plastic chair, trying to find a comfortable position as I stare down at my test booklet.

Question 17: *"A 65-year-old patient with hypertension and diabetes is currently taking lisinopril. Which of the following would be contraindicated?"*

I close my eyes briefly, taking a deep breath. The fluorescent lights hum overhead, matching the buzz of tension in my body. I know this. ACE inhibitors, diabetes... my mind races, flipping through mental flashcards.

A sudden vibration against my thigh makes me jump. My phone. I'd forgotten to turn it off completely. Panic floods through me as I fumble to silence it, my hands shaking. Sweat beads on my forehead as I pray the proctor hasn't noticed.

Heart pounding, I glance around the room. Other students are hunched over their papers, some frantically writing, others staring blankly ahead. The proctor paces slowly at the front of the room, her eyes scanning for any sign of cheating. I let out a shaky breath.

But now my concentration is shattered. Who was calling? Was it Dakota? Is he okay? Or worse, is he not okay?

Stop it, I tell myself firmly. *Focus. This exam is everything. Your future depends on it. Roman's future depends on it.*

I turn back to the question, willing my racing heart to slow. Contraindications for ACE inhibitors... The answer comes to me suddenly. Potassium-sparing diuretics. I fill in the bubble, a small surge of confidence flowing through me.

Question 18: *"List three potential side effects of beta-blockers."*

I start writing: *Fatigue, cold extremities, bradycardia...*

The clock on the wall ticks loudly, each second a

reminder of the time slipping away. Two hours left. My stomach churns as I realize I'm only a quarter of the way through the exam.

Question 19: *"Explain the mechanism of action for calcium channel blockers in the treatment of hypertension."*

I close my eyes, visualizing my textbook.

As I write the answer, I'm acutely aware of the pressure building behind my eyes, the beginnings of a stress headache. I roll my shoulders again, trying to release some tension.

A student two rows ahead stands up abruptly, startling me. They hand in their exam and leave. I glance at the clock again. How did they finish so quickly? Doubt creeps in. Am I going too slowly? Did I miss something?

No. Focus. One question at a time.

Question 20: *"A patient experiences a dry cough after starting a new hypertension medication. Which class of drugs is likely causing this side effect?"*

ACE inhibitors, I think, immediately. At least, that's straightforward.

As I move through the questions, time seems to both crawl and fly. My hand cramps from writing, and my eyes burn from the strain of reading. But I push through, each answered question a small victory.

The proctor's voice cuts through the silence: "One hour remaining."

Panic flares in my chest. I'm only halfway through. I force myself to breathe deeply, fighting the urge to rush. Rushing leads to mistakes. Mistakes lead to failure. And failure... failure isn't an option.

Not when I've worked so hard. Not when Roman's counting on me. Not when this degree is my ticket to a better life for us.

And maybe, a small voice whispers, *not when it might be the only stable thing in your life if things with Dakota fall apart.*

I push the thought aside, focusing on the next question. One at a time. I can do this. I have to.

The clock ticks on, a steady reminder that time, like everything else in my life right now, is running out. But I'm still here, still fighting. Still answering questions.

And for now, that has to be enough.

thirty-seven
alone in a room

Dakota

The tour bus rumbles beneath me, its familiar vibration doing little to calm my frayed nerves. Outside the window, an unfamiliar cityscape blurs by, all grey concrete and neon signs. My fingers drum an erratic rhythm on my thigh, muscle memory from countless bass lines. But today, it's anxiety, not music, directing the beat.

In my other hand, I clutch a crumpled piece of paper with an address scribbled on it. My first AA meeting in this new city. My throat tightens at the thought, and I swallow hard, tasting the bitter remnants of this morning's coffee.

"You sure about this?" Brad asks from the seat next to me. He's been my shadow lately, ever since I admitted I needed help. "We could run through the new set list one more time instead."

For a moment, I'm tempted. The thought of losing myself in music, in the familiar comfort of my bass, is almost overwhelming. But then I remember Lauren's voice on the phone, the disappointment and fear. I remember Roman's laughter, so pure and trusting. I can't let them down.

Not again.

I shake my head. "No, I need to do this. The show isn't for hours. I've got time."

The bus slows to a stop, and my heart rate speeds up in inverse proportion. Through the tinted windows, I can see a nondescript building with a sign that simply reads "Community Center." This is it.

"Want me to come with you?" Brad offers, his voice low.

For a moment, I'm tempted to say yes. To have someone there, a buffer between me and the raw vulnerability I'm about to face. But I shake my head. "I appreciate it, man, but... I think I need to do this on my own."

Brad nods, understanding. "Alright. I'll be here when you're done. And Dakota? I'm proud of you, man."

His words hit me harder than any power chord I've ever played. I swallow the lump in my throat and nod, not trusting myself to speak.

As I step off the bus, the humid air hits me like a wall, instantly plastering my t-shirt to my back. I take a deep breath, steeling myself. One foot in front of the other. Just like walking on stage, I tell myself. But this isn't a performance. This is real life, and the stakes are so much higher.

The community center smells of industrial cleaner and stale coffee. The fluorescent lights flicker overhead, casting harsh shadows. I follow the signs to a room at the end of the hall, my footsteps echoing in the empty corridor. Through the open door, I can see a circle of chairs. Some are already occupied.

My hands are shaking now, and I clench them into fists. What if someone recognizes me? What if this ends up online? What if I can't do this?

A memory surfaces: my first big show with Chaos Fuel. The paralyzing stage fright, the certainty that I was going to mess up. And then the first note, the rush of adrenaline, the realization that I belonged there.

"First time?"

I turn to see a middle-aged woman with kind eyes looking at me. She doesn't seem to recognize me, or if she does, she doesn't show it.

"Is it that obvious?" I manage a weak smile.

She shrugs. "We were all first-timers once. Come on in. We're about to start."

As I step into the room, I'm hit with a sense of déjà vu. How many green rooms have I walked into, feeling this same mix of anticipation and dread? But this isn't a show. This is my life.

I take a seat, the folding chair creaking under my weight. Around me, people chat quietly or sit in contemplative silence. Nobody gives me a second glance. Here, I'm not Dakota, the bassist of Chaos Fuel. I'm just another person trying to stay sober.

As the meeting begins, I close my eyes briefly. I think of Lauren, of Roman. Of the life I want to have with them. Of the man I want to be. I think of the music I want to make, clear-headed and honest.

And just like that, I've taken the first step on a new stage. The hardest performance of my life is about to begin. But for the first time in a long time, I feel ready to face it.

As the meeting leader, a man with salt-and-pepper hair and calloused hands that speak of hard-won sobriety asks if anyone would like to share, the air grows thick with anticipation.

My heart pounds a frantic rhythm in my chest, like a drum solo threatening to drown out everything else. I've stood before crowds of thousands, but this small circle of strangers terrifies me more than any stadium ever has.

A woman across from me starts speaking, her voice trembling slightly as she recounts her week. I try to focus, but my mind keeps drifting, like a guitar string that won't stay in tune. I think of the mini-bar in my hotel room, of the drink I almost had last night, of Lauren's face during our last video chat, what feels like forever ago – the softness in her features like lyrics I can't forget.

Before I know it, the woman has finished. The leader asks if anyone else would like to share. The silence stretches, punctuated only by the hum of the air conditioner and the occasional shuffle of feet. It's like that moment before a song starts, when the audience holds its breath in anticipation.

I take a deep breath. It's now or never. Time to face the music.

"I'd like to share," I hear myself say, my voice sounding strange to my own ears, like I'm listening to a recording of myself.

All eyes turn to me, but there's no judgment in their gazes. Just understanding. Acceptance. It's nothing like the scrutiny of fans or critics, and yet it feels more significant somehow.

"I'm Dakota," I begin, my mouth dry as sandpaper. "And I'm an alcoholic."

"Hi, Dakota," the group responds in unison, the chorus to my solo.

I swallow hard, pushing down the lump in my throat. My hands are shaking, and I clasp them tightly in my lap. "This is my first meeting. I'm... I'm on tour right now. I'm a musician. And I thought I could handle it, you know? The parties, the stress, the late nights. I thought I was different."

A memory flashes through my mind: my first backstage party, the rush of the performance still coursing through my veins, Chase pressing a drink into my hand. "To celebrate," he'd said. If only I'd known then where that celebration would lead.

"But I'm not different," I continue, my voice growing stronger. "I'm just like everyone else here. I have a problem, and I can't solve it on my own. I've hurt people I care about. I've put my career at risk. And I'm terrified that I'm going to lose everything if I don't get this under control."

My voice cracks on the last word, and I feel tears prickling at the corners of my eyes. But I push on, like playing through a broken string.

"I have a girlfriend, Lauren. And her son, Roman. They're... they're everything to me. And I want to be the man they deserve. The man I know I can be when I'm sober."

Another memory surfaces: Roman's laughter as I taught him how to hold a bass guitar, his small hands dwarfed by the instrument. The pure joy on his face mirrored in Lauren's eyes as she watched us. I want that moment back. I want a lifetime of moments like that.

"I don't know how to do this," I admit, my voice barely above a whisper. "How to stay sober on tour, how to face the pressure and the temptation. But I know I have to try. For them. But mostly for myself."

As I finish speaking, I feel a weight lift from my shoulders. It's not gone completely, but it's lighter. Manageable. Like setting down a heavy instrument after a long set.

The leader nods, a small smile on his face. "Thank you for sharing, Dakota. It takes courage to speak up, especially at your first meeting. Remember, we're all here for the same reason. You're not alone in this."

As the meeting continues, I feel a sense of calm wash over me. For the first time in weeks, maybe months, I feel... hope. It's small, fragile, but it's there. Like the first note of a new song, full of potential.

I may be on a different kind of tour now, but I'm

ready. One day at a time. One note at a time. And maybe, just maybe, I can compose a life worth living.

break me down

Lauren

The late afternoon sun shines across the countertop where I'm attempting to help Roman with his alphabet worksheet. My mind, however, is nowhere near the ABCs.

It's been three weeks since I asked Dakota for space. Three weeks of silence that feels both necessary and unbearable. I miss him. God, I miss him. But I know I needed this time to focus on myself, on Roman, on my studies.

A knock at the door startles me from my reverie.

"Mommy, someone's here!" Roman announces excitedly, always eager for visitors.

"I know, sweetie. Stay here and keep working on your letters, okay?"

I open the door to find a sleek, professional-looking woman standing on my porch. Her crisp suit and perfectly coiffed dark hair seem out of place in our modest neighborhood.

"Lauren Hudson?" she asks, her voice clipped and efficient.

I nod, suddenly self-conscious of my messy ponytail and the stain on my t-shirt from Roman's lunch.

"I'm Cassidy Townsend, the lawyer for Blackmore Records." She extends a hand, which I shake automatically, my mind reeling. Blackmore Records. Dakota's label.

"Is everything okay?" I ask, my heart rate picking up. "Is Dakota—"

"Dakota is fine," she interrupts smoothly, a gentleness and reassurance now in her voice. "I'm here on his behalf to deliver this." She holds out a large manila envelope, sealed and unmarked.

I take it. The weight of it surprises me. "What is it?"

"The police report he requested," Cassidy says, her expression now sympathetic. "He asked me to tell you that it's entirely up to you whether you want to open it or not. He'll respect your decision either way."

The police report. About Miles and Chloe. My hands start to shake slightly.

"Thank you," I manage to say.

Cassidy nods and hesitates briefly. "Take care, Lauren."

As she walks back to her car, I close the door, leaning against it for support. The envelope in my hands suddenly feels like it weighs a ton.

"Mommy?" Roman's voice pulls me back to reality. "Who was that lady?"

"Just... just someone delivering something for

Mommy," I say, trying to keep my voice steady. "How about we take a break from letters and watch a movie?"

Roman cheers, the alphabet forgotten, as I set up his favorite cartoon. But even as I sit next to him on the couch, my mind is elsewhere.

The envelope sits on the kitchen counter, a ticking time bomb of information. Do I want to know what's inside? Do I want to uncover the truth about Miles and Chloe? And what will it mean for Dakota and me if I do?

I think about Dakota, about the effort it must have taken to get this report, to respect my need for space and send it through a lawyer instead of coming himself. I think about the past few weeks and how I've thrown myself into my studies and into being there for Roman. How I've tried not to think about Dakota and failed miserably.

The truth is, I love him. Despite everything, despite my fears and doubts, I love him. But is love enough? Is it enough to overcome addiction, distance, and the ghosts of our pasts?

As Roman laughs at something on screen, I make a decision. I'll open the envelope. Whatever's inside, I'll face it. Because that's what I do now – I face things head-on, for myself and for Roman.

But not tonight. Tonight, I'll sit here with my son and enjoy this moment of peace. Tomorrow is soon enough to uncover the secrets of the past.

For now, I let myself remember Dakota's smile, and the sound of his laugh. I let myself hope that maybe, just maybe, we can find our way back to each other.

But first, I need to find my way back to myself.

The manila envelope sits on my kitchen table, its edges crisp and unmarked, a stark contrast to the scattered crayons and cheerios that surround it. I can almost feel its presence, a physical weight in the room.

My fingers drum an anxious rhythm on the worn wooden tabletop. The house is quiet, too quiet without Roman's chatter or the usual background noise of cartoons. The silence feels oppressive, amplifying the thoughts swirling in my head.

I need to talk this through with someone, and I know exactly who to call.

I dial Shannon's number, my hands shaking slightly. She picks up on the second ring.

"Lauren? Is everything okay?"

I let out a shaky breath. "Hey, Shan. I... I need some advice."

There's a rustling on the other end, and I can picture Shannon settling in for a serious conversation. "I'm all ears. What's going on?"

I explain about the envelope, about Cassidy's visit, about Dakota's message that it's my choice whether to open it or not. As I speak, I pace the kitchen, my bare feet cool against the linoleum floor.

"Wow," Shannon says when I finish. "That's... a lot. How are you feeling about all this?"

I laugh, but there's no humor in it. "Honestly? I feel

like I'm on a roller coaster. One minute, I'm curious and almost excited to finally know the truth. The next, I'm terrified of what I might find out."

"That's understandable," Shannon says softly. "It's a big decision."

"It's not just the envelope," I admit, sinking onto a kitchen chair. "It's Dakota, it's us. I miss him. God, I miss him so much it hurts sometimes. But I'm also still scared."

"Scared of what, exactly?"

I close my eyes, feeling the sting of tears. "Of getting hurt again. Of putting my heart on the line. Of falling in love with an addict."

"But Dakota's not Miles," Shannon points out again gently.

"I know that. Logically, I know that. But emotionally..." I trail off, unsure how to express the tangle of feelings in my chest.

"Lauren," Shannon's voice is firm but kind. "Can I be honest with you?"

"Always."

"I think you're using this envelope and the space between you and Dakota as an excuse. You're scared, and that's okay. But at some point, you have to decide if what you and Dakota have is worth the risk."

Her words hit me hard. I feel my chest tighten, my breath coming in short gasps. "You think I'm being a coward?"

"No," Shannon says firmly. "I think you're being human. But I also think you're stronger than you give yourself credit for. You've been through so much. You can handle this, too."

I wipe away a tear that's escaped down my cheek. "So, what do you think I should do?"

"I can't make that decision for you," Shannon says. "But if it were me? I'd wait until Dakota's back from tour. Then I'd sit down with him and open that envelope together. Whatever's inside, you'll face it as a team."

"But what if..." I start, then stop, swallowing hard.

"What if what?" Shannon prompts.

"What if what's inside changes everything? What if it ruins any chance Dakota and I have?"

Shannon is quiet for a moment. "Or what if it brings you closer? What if knowing the truth helps you both heal and move forward together?"

I hadn't considered that possibility. The thought sends a flutter of hope through my chest. "You really think that's possible?"

"I think anything's possible," Shannon says. "But you'll never know if you don't take the risk."

After we hang up, I look at the envelope again. My heart is racing, and I can feel a thin sheen of sweat on my palms. But for the first time since it arrived, the envelope doesn't feel like a ticking time bomb. Instead, it feels like... a possibility. A chance for truth, for healing, for moving forward.

I pick up my phone again, and before I can second-guess myself, I type out a text to Dakota.

> ME: Hey. I hope the tour is going well.
> When you're back, we should talk.
> About us, about the envelope, about
> everything. I miss you.

My finger hovers over the send button for a long moment. Then, taking a deep breath, I press it.

It's a small step, but it's a step forward.

thirty-nine
above it all

Dakota

The green room buzzes with pre-show energy. The worn leather couch creaks as Brad shifts his weight, tuning his guitar. The sharp scent of hair spray mingles with the earthy aroma of the herbal tea Stefan insists on before every performance. Somewhere down the hall, I can hear the muffled Incendiary Ink sound check, the bass thumping through the walls.

But all of this fades into the background as I stare at my phone, my heart pounding so hard I can feel it in my fingertips. Lauren's message glows on the screen.

> LAUREN: Hey. I hope the tour is going well. When you're back, we should talk. About us, about the envelope, about everything. I miss you.

I miss you.

Those three words send a jolt through my system, like striking a perfect chord after weeks of dissonance.

"Earth to Dakota," Brad's voice cuts through my thoughts. "You okay, man? You look like you've seen a ghost."

I look up, realizing the rest of the band is staring at me. My hands are shaking slightly, and I can feel a thin sheen of sweat on my forehead. "It's Lauren," I say, my voice hoarse. I clear my throat and try again. "She... she wants to talk when we get back."

Brad's face breaks into a grin. "That's great news, right?"

"Yeah," I nod, a mix of excitement and anxiety swirling in my stomach, making me feel slightly nauseous. "Yeah, it is."

As the guys congratulate me, I can't help but think about how much has changed since Lauren asked for space. Twenty-three days of sobriety. Eighteen shows across fifteen cities. Countless cups of terrible gas station coffee to stay awake on overnight drives between venues. Hours spent in hotel gyms, working out instead of drinking to cope with stress.

"You've earned this, Dakota," Stefan says, clapping me on the shoulder. "You've worked hard."

I nod, grateful for their support. They've been my rock through this journey, keeping me accountable, and cheering me on at every milestone of sobriety. Even when it meant skipping after-parties or dealing with my caffeine-fueled mood swings on long bus rides.

"Two minutes, guys!" our stage manager calls, poking her head into the green room.

I take a deep breath, trying to center myself. The

familiar pre-show jitters mingle with a new feeling – hope for the future. My stomach does a flip, part excitement, part nervousness.

"Hey," Emmett says as we line up to take the stage. The hallway smells of dust and old cigarette smoke, a scent I've come to associate with anticipation. "Whatever happens with Lauren, we're here for you. You know that, right?"

I nod, feeling a lump form in my throat. "I know. Thanks, guys. For everything."

As we step onto the stage, the roar of the crowd washes over us. The heat from the stage lights hits me immediately, and I can taste the metallic tang of adrenaline in my mouth. But tonight, it's not just the music that's driving me. It's the promise of what's waiting for me when this tour ends.

Two more weeks. Fourteen more days of staying strong, of taking it one day at a time. And then I'll be home. Home to face Lauren, to open that envelope if she wants, to start rebuilding what I almost lost.

I strike the first chord of our opening song, feeling the vibration travel up my arm, grounding me in the present. For the first time in a long time, I'm not just playing music.

I'm playing for my future. For Lauren. For us.

And I've never been more ready for an encore.

forty
leave a light on

Lauren

T he house is quiet, save for Roman's faint snores drifting from his bedroom. I curl deeper into the worn fabric of the couch, my celebratory glass of wine cool against my palm.

On the screen, Chaos Fuel performs their latest single. The thrumming bass line seems to sync with my heartbeat as the camera pans to Dakota. My breath catches. He looks... good. His fingers dance across the strings with practiced ease, his body swaying to the rhythm. There's a focus in his eyes I haven't seen in months, a clarity that makes my chest tighten with hope.

Sober, I think, the word tasting sweet on my tongue, like the crisp Chardonnay I sip.

I know their last show was yesterday, but I have no idea when he'll be back. His last text to me, weeks ago, was simple: "Okay. Miss you too." Since then, silence. The space I asked for respected to a fault.

A knock at the door startles me, the wine sloshing

dangerously close to the rim of my glass. I glance at the clock - 10:37 PM. Who could it be at this hour?

My heart racing, I open the door.

Dakota.

The contrast between the man on my screen moments ago and the one standing before me is stark. The Dakota in the video was a performer, confident and distant. This Dakota... he's real, immediate, and breathtaking.

His hair is slightly longer, tousled as if he's been running his hands through it nervously. His skin is sun-kissed from weeks on the road, a light stubble shadowing his jaw. But it's his eyes that capture me - clear, bright, and filled with a vulnerability that makes my heart ache.

I notice the slight tremor in his hands, the way he swallows hard. His T-shirt is wrinkled, like he's just pulled it from a suitcase. He smells faintly of coffee and the night air, not a trace of alcohol.

For a long moment, we just stare at each other, drinking in the sight. I'm acutely aware of my own appearance - pajama shorts and an old college t-shirt, my hair piled messily atop my head. I wonder what he sees in me - the dark circles under my eyes from late-night study sessions? The new highlights in my hair I got on a whim last week?

Neither of us speaks. We don't need to.

In an instant, we're in each other's arms. His embrace is familiar yet new, strong, and sure. I feel the solid warmth of his body, the steady thump of his heart against my cheek. My fingers curl into the fabric of his shirt as if afraid he might disappear if I let go.

We stand there, holding each other, for what feels like hours. All the worry, the fear, the longing of the past months pours out in that embrace. I feel tears prick at my eyes, and I can feel Dakota's uneven breath against my hair, causing a shiver to run down my spine.

My body seems to melt into his, the tension of the past months - the stress of exams, the worry about his sobriety, the uncertainty of our future - ebbing away with each passing second.

There's so much to say, so much to discuss. The envelope. The tour. My school. Our future.

But for now, this is enough. This silent reunion, this wordless understanding.

We're here. We're together. And for the first time in a long time, it feels like everything might just be okay.

forty-one
i'm coming home

Dakota

The car feels suffocating as I pull up to Lauren's house. My hands shake slightly as I turn off the engine, and I take a deep breath, trying to steady myself. I've been rehearsing what to say for weeks, but now that I'm here, all the words seem to evaporate.

The porch light casts a warm glow on the familiar front door. How many times have I walked through it, feeling like I was coming home? Now, I'm not sure if I still have that right.

I check my reflection in the rearview mirror. My hair's a bit longer, and my face leaner after months of trading booze for workouts. I look better, I know. But will it be enough?

Before I can talk myself out of it, I'm out of the car and knocking on the door. The sound seems too loud in the quiet neighborhood.

For a moment, there's silence. Then, footsteps.

The door opens, and there she is.

Lauren.

My breath catches in my throat. She looks... tired. Beautiful, always beautiful, but exhausted. There are dark circles under her eyes, and her hair is piled messily on top of her head. She's wearing pajama shorts and an old T-shirt that I recognize as one I used to sleep in.

But it's her eyes that captivate me. They're wide with surprise, and beneath the fatigue, there's a spark. A glimmer of... hope? Happiness?

For a long moment, we just stare at each other. I drink in the sight of her, noticing small changes. New highlights in her hair. A small scrape on her knee, probably from chasing after Roman. She looks like she's carrying the weight of the world on her shoulders, but somehow, impossibly, she also looks happy to see me.

I open my mouth to speak, but no words come out. What can I say? *I'm sorry? I've missed you? I love you?*

Before I can figure it out, Lauren moves. In an instant, we're in each other's arms.

I pull her close, breathing in her scent. She smells like home - a hint of floral shampoo, the faint sweetness of wine on her breath. I can feel her heartbeat against my chest, quick and strong.

We stand there, holding each other, for what feels like forever. I pour every emotion into this hug. I feel a lump form in my throat, and I have to blink back tears.

Lauren's fingers curl into my shirt, and I tighten my arms around her. I want to memorize this moment, the feeling of her in my arms again.

There's so much to talk about. But as I hold her, I make a silent promise to her, to myself, to us. Whatever comes next, whatever challenges we face, I'm all in.

Because this - Lauren in my arms, the possibility of a future together - this is worth fighting for.

forty-two
iris

Lauren

W e finally pull apart, though I feel the loss of Dakota's warmth immediately. There's an awkward moment where we both just stand there, not quite meeting each other's eyes.

"Do you want to come in?" I ask, my voice sounding strange to my own ears.

Dakota nods, a small smile playing at the corners of his mouth. "Yeah, I'd like that."

I lead him to the kitchen, hyperaware of his presence behind me. The house suddenly feels different with him in it, like it's holding its breath. The soft ticking of the clock on the wall seems louder than usual, marking each second of this surreal moment.

"Can I get you something to drink?" I offer, then immediately freeze. The half-empty wine glass on the coffee table catches my eye, and guilt washes over me. I quickly move to hide it, my hands shaking slightly. "I mean, I have water, or soda, or..."

"Water would be great," Dakota says softly, and I can hear the understanding in his voice. His eyes follow my movement, but he doesn't comment on the wine.

As I fill a glass at the sink, I can feel Dakota's eyes on me. The cool water over my hands helps ground me, and gives me a moment to collect my thoughts. When I turn back, he's leaning against the counter, his posture relaxed but his eyes intense.

"So," I start, handing him the water. Our fingers brush, and I feel a jolt of electricity at the contact. "How was the tour?"

A smile breaks across his face, genuine and bright. "It was... incredible. Challenging, but incredible."

I nod, thinking of the video I was just watching. "I actually just saw a clip from one of your shows. From a couple weeks ago, I think?"

Dakota's eyebrows raise in surprise. "You were watching our videos?"

I feel a blush creep up my neck. "Yeah, I... I wanted to see how you were doing." I pause, gathering courage. "You looked good up there. Really good. Happy. Focused."

"I am," he says, his voice low and earnest. He sets down his glass and takes a step closer to me. "I've been working hard. Not just on the music, but on myself. On my sobriety."

The word hangs between us, full of weight and promise. I can smell his familiar scent - a mix of soap and something uniquely Dakota. It takes all my willpower not to close the distance between us.

"How long?" I ask, barely above a whisper.

"Thirty-eight days," he replies without hesitation. "Not that I'm counting or anything," he adds with a self-deprecating smile.

I feel tears prick in my eyes. "I'm proud of you, Dakota."

His eyes soften, and he reaches out, his hand hovering near my face as if he wants to wipe away a tear but isn't sure if he's allowed. "I couldn't have done it without thinking of you. Of us."

My heart races at his proximity. There's still so much to discuss, so much uncertainty. The envelope sits on my desk, a ticking time bomb of potential truths. But at this moment, all I can think about is how right it feels to have him here.

"Dakota, I—" I start, but the words catch in my throat. How do I express everything I'm feeling? The pride, the fear, the hope, the love?

He waits patiently, his eyes never leaving mine. In them, I see a reflection of my own emotions - uncertainty, yes, but also determination. And underneath it all, a love that never really went away.

"I missed you," I finally manage, the words feeling inadequate but true.

Dakota's smile is soft, tender. "I missed you too. More than I can say."

As we stand there, my eyes inadvertently drift to my desk in the corner of the living room. The envelope sits there, partially hidden under a stack of nursing textbooks. Dakota follows my gaze, his body tensing slightly as he spots it.

"Is that...?" he asks, his voice trailing off.

I nod, swallowing hard. "Yeah. I haven't opened it."

Dakota takes a deep breath, his fingers tapping an anxious rhythm on the countertop. "Do you want to?"

The question hangs in the air between us, heavy with implications. I bite my lip, considering my words carefully.

"I don't know," I admit. "Part of me wants to know the truth, but another part..." I hesitate, looking at Dakota. "I'm more worried about how it might affect you."

His brow furrows. "What do you mean?"

I take a deep breath, steeling myself. "Dakota, I... I knew Miles had been unfaithful before. Not at the end, but earlier in our relationship. The possibility that he was with someone else when he died, it's painful, but it's not entirely shocking."

Understanding dawns in Dakota's eyes. "But for me, with Chloe, it would be completely unexpected."

I nod, watching his face carefully. "Yeah. I guess I'm worried about how you'd handle that, if it turns out to be true."

Dakota is quiet for a moment, his gaze distant. When he speaks, his voice is soft but steady. "I've had a lot of time to think about this. About Chloe, about our marriage, about who she really was."

He looks at me, his eyes clear and focused. "The truth is, I don't know if I ever really knew her. Not completely.

And while the idea of her being unfaithful hurts, I think... I think I've come to terms with the possibility."

I feel a mix of relief and sadness wash over me. "How did you get there?"

Dakota runs a hand through his hair, a gesture so familiar it makes my heart ache. "It wasn't easy. But part of my recovery has been about facing hard truths. About myself, about my relationships. And the more I thought about it, the more I realized that Chloe and I... we weren't in a good place long before she died."

He takes a step closer to me, his voice low and intense. "Lauren, whatever's in that envelope, it doesn't change how I feel about you. About us. If anything, it might give us both the closure we need to move forward. Together, if that's what you want."

My breath catches in my throat. "Is that what you want?"

Dakota's eyes meet mine, unwavering. "More than anything."

I nod, feeling a surge of courage. "Then I think we should open it. Together."

Dakota reaches out, taking my hand in his. The warmth of his touch sends a shiver through me. "Together," he agrees.

As we move towards the desk, I feel a mix of anxiety and anticipation. Whatever truths that envelope holds, we're about to face them. And for the first time, I truly believe we can handle it.

Because we're doing it together.

forty-three
dream away

Dakota

My heart pounds in my chest as Lauren carefully opens the envelope. The sound of tearing paper seems impossibly loud in the quiet room. I hold my breath, watching her unfold the document inside.

Her eyes scan the page, widening slightly. I see a range of emotions flicker across her face – surprise, pain, confusion.

"Dakota," she says softly, looking up at me. "It's... it's true. They were together."

Even though I've tried to prepare myself for this moment, the confirmation hits me like a physical blow. I feel a sharp pain in my chest, and for a moment, the room seems to spin.

Lauren continues, her voice gentle. "The report names both Miles and Chloe. They were found together in... in a hotel room."

I close my eyes, trying to steady myself. Images of

Chloe flash through my mind – her smile, her laugh, the way she looked on our wedding day. Had it all been a lie?

"There are other names, too," Lauren adds, drawing my attention back. "Witnesses, I think."

I nod, not trusting myself to speak yet. My mind is racing, trying to process this information. Chloe, my wife, the woman I thought I knew, had been living a double life. And I had been completely blind to it.

"Dakota?" Lauren's voice is laced with concern. "Are you okay?"

I take a deep breath, finally opening my eyes to meet her gaze. "I... I don't know," I admit. "It hurts. More than I thought it would."

Lauren reaches out, her hand warm on my arm. "I'm so sorry."

Her touch grounds me, reminding me that I'm not alone in this. I cover her hand with mine, grateful for her presence.

"It's not your fault," I say. "And in a way... it's almost a relief."

Lauren looks surprised. "A relief?"

I nod slowly, the realization dawning as I speak. "Yeah. All this time, I've been wondering, imagining different scenarios. But now we know. It's... it's closure, I guess."

The pain is still there, a dull ache in my chest. But alongside it, I feel something else – a weight lifting, a fog clearing.

"I spent so long idolizing Chloe after she died," I continue, the words pouring out now. "Blaming myself for not being a better husband, for not saving her. But this... this shows that she made her own choices. Choices that had nothing to do with me."

Lauren listens intently, her eyes never leaving mine. "That must be a lot to process."

I nod, feeling unshed tears sting my eyes. "It is. But it also feels like... like I can finally start to let go. To move on."

My gaze falls on our joined hands, then back to Lauren's face. In her eyes, I see understanding, compassion, and something else – hope.

"Lauren," I say, my voice thick with emotion. "I know this is a lot. For both of us. But I meant what I said before. This doesn't change how I feel about you. About us."

She squeezes my hand gently. "I feel the same way."

For the first time since the envelope was opened, I feel a smile tugging at my lips. The pain of Chloe's betrayal is still fresh, but it's overshadowed by the warmth of Lauren's presence, the promise of a future together.

"So," I say, my voice steadier now. "Where do we go from here?"

Lauren's smile mirrors my own. "Forward," she says simply. "Together."

And in that moment, I know that whatever difficulties lie ahead, we'll face them side by side. The truth, as painful as it is, has set us free. And I'm ready to embrace that freedom with Lauren by my side.

forty-four
my underworld

Lauren

As Dakota and I talk, our voices low and intimate, the weight of the day, of our reunion, of everything we've learned, settles over me like a blanket. I feel my eyelids growing heavy, Dakota's heartbeat a soothing rhythm beneath my ear.

"Lauren?" His voice is gentle, far away. "I think you're falling asleep."

I mumble something incoherent, burrowing closer into his warmth. I feel his chuckle rumble through his chest.

"Come on," he says softly. "Let's get you to bed."

Strong arms lift me, and I instinctively wrap my own around his neck. His familiar scent envelops me as he carries me to the bedroom.

As he lays me down, our eyes meet in the dim light. The tenderness in his gaze makes my breath catch.

"Stay," I whisper, my hand finding his.

For a moment, he hesitates. Then, with a soft smile, he nods.

Our lips meet softly at first, then with increasing urgency. Months of longing, of missing each other, pour into every touch. Dakota's hands trail down my sides, leaving goosebumps in their wake. I arch into him, craving more contact.

Clothes are shed slowly, reverently, each newly exposed inch of skin explored with fingers and lips. Dakota's body is familiar yet new - more toned from his time on tour, a map I'm eager to rediscover.

When he finally enters me, we both gasp. The feeling of completeness, of coming home, is overwhelming. We move together, finding our rhythm easily, as if we'd never been apart.

"God, I've missed you," Dakota murmurs against my neck, his voice thick with emotion.

I can only nod, too overcome to speak. My fingers dig into his back, pulling him closer, deeper.

Our pace quickens, driven by months of pent-up desire. I feel the tension building, coiling tighter and tighter until, finally, it snaps. I cry out Dakota's name as waves of pleasure wash over me. He follows soon after, his face buried in my hair as he shudders against me.

In the aftermath, we lie tangled together, my head on his chest, his fingers tracing lazy patterns on my back. The world outside fades away, leaving only this moment, only us.

"I love you," Dakota murmurs into my hair.

I tilt my head up to meet his gaze, seeing in his eyes everything I feel reflected back at me. "I love you, too."

As sleep begins to claim me once more, I feel a sense of peace settle over me.

We're home.

forty-five
i've found

Dakota

When I rouse from sleep, for a moment, I'm disoriented, but then I feel Lauren's warm body pressed against mine, and everything clicks into place. I'm home.

I glance at the clock on the nightstand - 6:15 AM. We need to get up before Roman wakes and realizes I spent the night. As much as I want to stay in this moment forever, I know we need to be careful for Roman's sake.

"Lauren," I whisper, gently stroking her arm. "We should get up."

She stirs, her eyes fluttering open. A slow smile spreads across her face as she sees me, and my heart swells.

"Good morning," she murmurs, leaning in for a soft kiss.

We dress quickly and quietly, stealing glances and shy smiles. It feels like we're teenagers again, sneaking around. But there's an undercurrent of seriousness, too -

we both know we need to handle this situation delicately for Roman's sake.

I'm in the kitchen, starting the coffee maker, when I hear the patter of small feet.

"Dakota!" Roman's excited voice rings out. Before I know it, he's launched himself at me, and I scoop him up in a big hug.

"Hey, buddy!" I say, my heart full. "I missed you!"

Lauren appears in the doorway, her eyes soft as she watches us. "Look who came over early to help with breakfast," she says to Roman, smoothly covering for my presence.

Roman's face lights up. "Can we have pancakes? Please?"

I look at Lauren, who nods with a smile. "Pancakes it is," I declare.

The morning unfolds in a whirl of flour, giggles, and sticky syrup. As I flip pancakes and listen to Roman chatter about his daycare adventures, I'm struck by how right this feels. This is what I've been missing, what I've been working so hard for.

After breakfast, we decide to spend the day at the park. Roman runs ahead, his energy seemingly boundless, while Lauren and I walk hand in hand behind him.

"Is this okay?" I ask softly, squeezing her hand. "Me being here, spending the day with you both?"

Lauren looks up at me, her eyes clear and sure. "It's more than okay, Dakota. It's perfect."

We spend hours at the park, pushing Roman on the

swings, helping him across the monkey bars, and having a picnic lunch on a sunny patch of grass. As the afternoon wears on, Roman's energy finally starts to flag.

"I think it's time to head home," Lauren says, noticing Roman's yawns.

On the walk back, Roman insists on riding on my shoulders. His small hands rest on my head, and I hold onto his legs, ensuring he's secure. Lauren walks beside us, her hand occasionally brushing against mine.

Back at the house, Roman is barely awake. "Can Dakota tuck me in?" he asks sleepily.

Lauren and I exchange a glance. "Of course, buddy," I say, my throat tight with emotion.

As I tuck Roman into bed, he looks up at me with heavy-lidded eyes. "I'm glad you're back, Dakota," he mumbles.

"Me too, buddy," I whisper, smoothing his hair. "Me too."

When I return to the living room, Lauren is waiting for me on the couch. I sit next to her, and she immediately curls into my side.

"Thank you for today," she says softly.

I press a kiss to the top of her head. "No, thank you. For giving me another chance. For letting me be a part of your lives again."

Lauren looks up at me, her eyes shining. "Our lives, Dakota. You're a part of our lives."

As we sit there, the evening light fades around us, and I feel a sense of peace I haven't known in months. There's still a lot to figure out, I know. But right here, right now, with Lauren in my arms and Roman sleeping peacefully down the hall, I know I'm exactly where I'm supposed to be.

forty-six
you are in love

Lauren

The kitchen table is covered in textbooks and notes, my laptop screen glowing with half-finished flashcards. I rub my eyes, trying to focus on the intricate details of cellular respiration. From the living room, I hear the muffled sounds of a cartoon, punctuated by Roman's giggles and Dakota's deep chuckle.

I can't help but smile. This has become our new normal over the past few weeks - me studying while Dakota and Roman have their "guy time" before bed. It's a rhythm we've fallen into naturally, and it works.

Glancing up from my notes, I catch Dakota's eye over Roman's head. He gives me a soft smile, one that still makes my heart skip a beat. I return it, feeling a warmth spread through my chest. We've come so far in such a short time.

As the cartoon ends, Dakota stretches and ruffles Roman's hair. "Alright, buddy. Time for bed."

"Aww, can't we watch one more?" Roman pleads, his best puppy-dog eyes on full display.

Dakota chuckles, immune to the charm. "Nice try, but you know the rules. Come on, let's get you tucked in."

After Roman gives me a kiss goodnight, I watch as Dakota scoops him up, my son's laughter echoing down the hallway. The sound of their voices fades as they disappear into Roman's room, leaving me with a moment of quiet.

I try to return to my studies but find myself straining to hear their muffled conversation instead. After a few minutes, Dakota's voice becomes clearer, and I realize he's telling Roman a bedtime story.

"Once upon a time," Dakota begins, his voice taking on a playful, theatrical tone, "there was a brave knight named Sir Roman the Fearless..."

I can't help but smile, imagining Roman's wide-eyed excitement at being the hero of the tale. Dakota weaves a fantastical story of dragons and magical quests, his voice rising and falling with the action. I find myself drawn in, my studies forgotten as I listen to the adventure unfold.

As the story comes to a close, I hear Dakota's voice soften. "And Sir Roman returned home, where he was greeted by his loving family. They were so proud of his bravery and kindness. The end."

There's a moment of silence, then Roman's sleepy voice: "That was a good story, Dakota. Can you tell me another one tomorrow?"

"You bet, buddy," Dakota replies. "Sweet dreams."

I quickly return to my books as I hear Dakota's footsteps approaching. He enters the kitchen, a soft smile on his face.

"He's out like a light," Dakota says, coming to stand behind me. His hands rest on my shoulders, gently massaging the tension away. "How's the studying going?"

I lean back into his touch, sighing contentedly. "It's going. Though I have to admit, I got a bit distracted by Sir Roman's adventure."

Dakota chuckles, leaning down to press a kiss to the top of my head. "What can I say? I'm a man of many talents."

I turn in my chair to face him, reaching up to cup his cheek. "You certainly are. Thank you for being so amazing with him."

Dakota's eyes soften, his hand covering mine. "Lauren, you don't have to thank me. I love that little guy. And I love you."

The sincerity in his voice makes my heart swell. "I love you too," I whisper.

As Dakota leans down to kiss me, I'm struck by how right this feels. The three of us are building this life together. It hasn't always been easy, and I know we still have challenges ahead. But moments like these - Dakota's bedtime stories, Roman's laughter, the quiet intimacy between us - they make it all worth it.

I deepen the kiss, my studies forgotten for now. There will be time for cellular respiration later. Right now, I just want to savor this moment, this feeling of family, of all-encompassing love that I've only dreamed of.

forty-seven
otherside

Dakota

T he familiar scent of coffee and cookies fills the community center as I take a seat in the circle. A few faces nod politely in my direction. It's been several weeks since I've been to a meeting, and this is a brand new group to me.

"Welcome, everyone," the group leader, a middle-aged man with kind eyes, begins. "I'm Tom. Let's start with introductions. Who'd like to go first?"

Before I can second-guess myself, I raise my hand. Tom nods encouragingly.

"Hi, I'm Dakota," I begin, my voice steadier than I feel. "And I'm an alcoholic."

"Hi, Dakota," the group responds in unison.

I take a deep breath, centering myself. "I'm... not usually at this meeting. I've been on tour with my band, but I'm back in town now. A lot has happened, and I felt like I needed to share, if that's okay."

Tom nods. "Of course, Dakota. This is a safe space. Please, go ahead."

I nod, grateful for the encouragement. "Recently, I found out some difficult truths about my late wife, Chloe. It turns out she was... unfaithful. She died alongside the man she was having an affair with."

A few sympathetic murmurs ripple through the group, but no one interrupts.

"The thing is," I continue, "I was surprised by how well I handled it. Don't get me wrong, it hurt. It still hurts. But it didn't send me spiraling like I feared it might. I didn't reach for a drink. Instead, I reached out to my support system. To Lauren, my... my girlfriend."

I pause, realizing I've never referred to Lauren that way out loud before. It feels right.

"Lauren is... well, she's incredible. She's been by my side through all of this. We're building something real, something strong. And her son, Roman... he's amazing. Being with them, it feels like I've found my place in the world."

I look around the circle, making brief eye contact with a few attentive faces. "I guess what I'm trying to say is, I'm grateful. Grateful for my sobriety, for the clarity it's given me. Grateful for second chances. And grateful for groups like this, for giving me a place to work through all of this."

As I finish speaking, I feel a weight lift from my shoulders. Sharing this, acknowledging how far I've come, feels significant.

Tom nods, a warm smile on his face. "Thank you for

sharing, Dakota. It takes courage to face difficult truths, and even more courage to share them with strangers. Does anyone else have any thoughts they'd like to add?"

A woman across the circle raises her hand. "I just want to say, Dakota, that your story gives me hope. To hear how you've handled such a difficult situation without turning to alcohol... it's inspiring. Thank you."

Others nod in agreement, and I feel a warmth spread through my chest. This is why I keep coming to these meetings, even in unfamiliar places. The understanding, the support, and the shared journey toward recovery.

As the meeting continues, I listen to others share their stories, their struggles, and their triumphs. Each one resonates with me in some way, reminding me that I'm not alone in this journey.

When the meeting ends, I stand awkwardly for a moment, unsure whether to linger or leave. Tom approaches me.

"It's good to have you here, Dakota," he says warmly. "I hope we'll see you again."

I nod, feeling a mix of gratitude and shyness. "Thanks, Tom. I'll try to come back when I can."

As I walk to my car, I pull out my phone. There's a text from Lauren.

> LAUREN: Hope the meeting went well. Roman and I are making spaghetti. See you soon. Love you.

I smile, typing out a quick reply:

ME: It was great. Can't wait to see you both. Love you too.

Driving to Lauren's - because it's become more of a home than my own place - I feel a sense of peace wash over me. Life isn't perfect. There are still challenges, still moments of doubt. But for the first time in a long fucking time, I feel equipped to handle whatever comes my way.

One day at a time, one step at a time. With Lauren and Roman by my side, I'm ready to face it all.

epilogue 1

Believe in Yourself

Lauren – Three Years Later

The auditorium buzzes with excitement as I adjust my cap one last time. My palms are sweaty, but it's not from nerves. It's anticipation. Pride. Joy.

I scan the crowd, searching for the faces that matter most. There, in the third row - Dakota, Roman, and Shannon. My family, both chosen and born.

Dakota catches my eye and grins, giving me a thumbs up. Roman, now six and growing like a weed, waves enthusiastically. Shannon, who flew in from Seattle just for this, blows me a kiss. I wave back, my heart swelling with love.

Three years. Three intense years of late nights studying, of juggling clinicals and motherhood, of building a life with Dakota. It hasn't always been easy, but we've made it. Together.

As I wait for my name to be called, my mind drifts

back to where we started. The broken pieces we've put back together. The trust we've rebuilt. The love that's grown stronger with every challenge we've faced.

Dakota's sobriety journey has mirrored my nursing school path - about three years now. It hasn't been perfect, but he's committed, attending meetings regularly and working hard every day. Chaos Fuel is thriving, too, finding a balance between touring and home life that works for all of us.

"Lauren Hudson," the dean calls.

I step forward, my gown swishing around my ankles. As I accept my diploma, I hear familiar voices rise above the applause.

"Way to go, Mom!" "You did it, Lauren!"

Then, clear as day, I hear it. A moment I'll cherish forever.

"Dad, did you see? Mom did it!"

Dad. Roman called Dakota 'Dad.'

My eyes find my little group again. Roman's standing on his chair, Dakota's hands on his shoulders to steady him, both of them beaming with pride. Dakota's eyes are wide with surprise and joy, glistening with unshed tears. Shannon's on her feet, cheering loudly, happy tears streaming down her face.

By the time I make it back to them, Dakota's composure is mostly back, but his eyes are still shining.

"Congratulations, Nurse Hudson," he says, pulling me into a hug. "We're so proud of you."

"Mom, you were awesome!" Roman chimes in, wrapping his arms around my waist.

Shannon engulfs us all in a hug. "I knew you could do it, girl. I'm so proud of you."

I kneel down to Roman's level, cupping his face in my hands. "Thank you, sweetheart. I couldn't have done it without all of you cheering me on."

Roman grins, then looks up at Dakota. "Can we have ice cream to celebrate? Please, Dad?"

There it is again. *Dad*. It sounds so right.

Dakota meets my gaze over Roman's head, love and wonder clear in his eyes. "What do you think? Ice cream sound good to you?"

I nod, too choked up to speak. Instead, I pull them all into a group hug, my cap going askew in the process.

We head to the car, Roman chattering excitedly about his ice cream plans, and Shannon and Dakota discuss dinner options. As we walk, Dakota leans in close to me.

"I have a surprise for you later," he whispers. "Let's just say, I think it's time we made this family official. If you'll have me, that is."

My heart skips a beat as I realize what he's implying. I squeeze his hand, a silent yes.

Our story isn't over. In many ways, it feels like it's just beginning. But whatever comes next, I know we'll face it together - me, Dakota, Roman, and Shannon supporting us from wherever she is. Our little family, stronger than ever.

Standing here, with my nursing degree in hand and my favorite people by my side, I know one thing for certain: This is our happily ever after. It's not perfect, but it's real, it's ours, and it's better than anything I could have dreamed.

epilogue 2

I Was Made for Lovin' You

Dakota

The house is quiet as I slip out of bed, careful not to wake Lauren. She's exhausted from the excitement of graduation, but I can't sleep. My heart is racing with anticipation.

In the kitchen, I pull out the small velvet box I've been hiding for weeks. The ring inside catches the moonlight, and I can't help but smile. It's time.

My mind drifts back to earlier today, before the graduation ceremony...

"So, what do you think?" I asked, showing the ring to Shannon.

Her eyes widened, a grin spreading across her face. "Dakota, it's beautiful. She's going to love it."

"You think she'll say yes?"

Shannon laughed, punching my arm lightly. "Are you kidding? Of course, she will. You two are perfect for each other."

I nodded, trying to quell the butterflies in my stomach. "There's one more person I need to ask."

We found Roman in the living room, engrossed in a video. I knelt beside him, my heart pounding.

"Hey, buddy. Can I ask you something important?"

Roman paused his video, looking at me curiously. "What is it?"

I took a deep breath. "Roman, you know I love you and your mom very much, right?"

He nodded.

"Well, I was wondering... how would you feel if I asked your mom to marry me? If I became your dad officially?"

Roman's eyes widened. For a moment, he was quiet, and I felt my heart stop. Then, he launched himself at me, wrapping his arms around my neck.

"Really? You want to be my dad?"

I hugged him back, feeling tears well in my eyes. "More than anything, buddy."

"Then yes!" Roman exclaimed. "You have to ask her, Dad!"

Dad. The word filled me with joy every time I heard it.

Now, as I stand in the moonlit kitchen, those moments

give me strength. I head back to the bedroom, ring in hand, ready to start the next chapter of our lives.

Lauren is just stirring as I enter. She blinks sleepily, a soft smile on her face. "Dakota? What's going on?"

I sit on the edge of the bed, taking her hand in mine. "Lauren, I love you. You and Roman... you've given me a family, a home. I want to spend the rest of my life with you."

I open the ring box, my heart pounding. "Will you marry me?"

Lauren's eyes widen, glistening with tears in the dim light. For a moment, there's silence. Then she nods, a radiant smile spreading across her face.

"Yes," she whispers. "Yes, of course I'll marry you."

As I slip the ring onto her finger and pull her into a kiss, I'm overwhelmed with gratitude. This is my family. My home. My happily ever after.

And it's only the beginning.

- THE END -

madness playlist

https://rebrand.ly/on316re

1. *Nothing Ever After* – Illenium, Motionless in White
2. *Holding Out for a Hero*, Nothing but Thieves
3. *Light in Life*, Silvera
4. *Blackbird,* Joseph Vincent
5. *The Prophecy,* Taylor Swift
6. *Spirits High,* The Exies
7. *Beach Seduction,* The Picturebooks, Leah Wellbaum
8. *Fall Eternal,* Black Veil Brides
9. *Time is Running Out,* Muse
10. *Help,* Hurts
11. *Stay Away,* Night Darling
12. *Remember Me,* Embrace
13. *Drive,* Incubus
14. *Power Over Me,* Dermot Kennedy
15. *Dear Prudence,* Siouxsie and the Banshees

16. *All You Need Is Love,* Jim Sturgess, Dana Fuchs
17. *Miss Independent,* Kelly Clarkson
18. *Here For Good,* Failure Anthem
19. *Passacaglia,* Bear McCreary
20. *Kiss from a Rose,* Wake Me
21. *Goddess,* PVRIS
22. *Coincidences,* Rich Beeston
23. *Stick Around,* The Luka State
24. *NFWMB,* Hozier
25. *I Miss You,* Incubus
26. *Barely Alive,* Oceans Divide
27. *Why Do I Even Try,* Plush
28. *Hopeless,* Picturesque
29. *Terrible Things,* Halestorm
30. *Heart of Novocaine,* Halestorm
31. *Animals,* Architects
32. *In the Air Tonight,* Natalie Taylor
33. *Adrenaline,* Zero 9:36
34. *I Feel It Too,* Dream State
35. *The Jester,* Badflower
36. *The Unknown,* 10 Years
37. *Alone in a Room,* Asking Alexandria
38. *Break Me Down,* Red
39. *Above It All,* Archetypes Collide
40. *Leave a Light On,* Papa Roach
41. *I'm Coming Home,* Jared Benjamin
42. *Iris,* Diamante, Breaking Benjamin
43. *Dream Away,* Keith Wallen

44. *My Underworld,* Tonight Alive, Corey Taylor
45. *I've Found,* Dokken
46. *You Are in Love,* Taylor Swift
47. *Otherside,* Ayron Jones
48. *Believe in Yourself,* War & Peace
49. *I Was Made for Lovin' You,* Yungblud, Dominic Lewis

bonus song – mayhem and madness

Verse 1:

In the mayhem of my mind
Searching for a peace I can't find
You're the calm in this storm inside
The spark that keeps my fire alive

Chorus:

Madness and magic intertwined
Your love, the remedy I need
In this world so undefined
You're the only sanity I see

Verse 2:

Fueling the flames that burn so bright
Your touch turns darkness into light

In this dance of shadow and shade
You're the balance that I've made

(Repeat Chorus)
Bridge:

Through the mayhem, through the
    madness
You're my anchor, you're my compass
In this wild symphony
You're the melody that sets me free

(Repeat Chorus)
Outro:

In the mayhem, in the madness
You're the fuel that keeps me breathing

bonus song – midnight mirage

Verse 1:

City lights blur in the rain
Neon signs, they spell your name
Chasing shadows down these streets
A phantom love I'll never meet

Chorus:

Midnight mirage, you're just out of reach
A beautiful lie I can't seem to breach
Fading away with the coming dawn
Midnight mirage, and then you're gone

Verse 2:

Whiskey dreams and smoky bars
Trying to forget who you are

But your memory lingers still
A ghostly touch, a silent thrill

(Repeat Chorus)
Bridge:

In the twilight between truth and illusion
You dance on the edge of my confusion
Real or imagined, I can't let you go
This midnight mirage is all I know

(Repeat Chorus)
Outro:

As the sun rises, you disappear
Leaving me alone with my fear
Midnight mirage, was it all in my head?
Or the love I lost, now cold and dead?

Thank you

If you enjoyed this book, please consider taking a moment to leave a Review. Even a star Rating helps indie authors reach a wider audience.

goodreads   amazon kindle   BookBub

also by amy booker

Near Miss Rock Star Series

Almost

So Close

Barely

Near Miss Rock Star Collection

In Reach

Drive Me Wild Vegas Series

Ms. Fortune

Ms. Chief

Ms. Lead

Ms. Take

The Mischief Motors Collection

Rhapsody Rock Star Series

Coda

Reprise

Overture

Waltz

Sustain

Chaos Fuel Rock Star Series

Mayhem

contact amy

Follow

My website: http://www.amybookerauthor.com
Facebook: www.facebook.com/amybookerauthor
Instagram: www.instagram.com/amy_booker_author/
TikTok: www.TikTok.com/@amybookerauthor
Goodreads: www.goodreads.com/author/show/
22225202.Amy_Booker
Amazon: https://rebrand.ly/sraegoj

Buy Direct

Amy Booker Store: https://payhip.com/AmyBooker

Interact

Email: amybookerauthor@gmail.com
Facebook Reader Group: https://www.facebook.com/
groups/amybookersroadies
Newsletter Sign Up: https://www.amybookerauthor.
com/subscribe

Read Early

Join my ARC Team: https://forms.gle/Ns1QKmrrs
Qz4ay5S6